Write Michigan 2023 Anthology

Chapbook Press

Schuler Books
2660 28th Street SE
Grand Rapids, MI 49512
(616) 942-7330
www.schulerbooks.com

Write Michigan 2023 Anthology

ISBN 13: 9781957169415

Molly Bilbey

Katherine Blackwell

Aubrey Borr

Erin Burchill

Riley Carey

Emilee Ceuninck

Chris Cochran

Ensley DeYonker

Yolihuani Dietachmayr

Faith Grimmet

Caitlin Horrocks

Emma Katke

Malachi King

Cassie Peckens

Sara Proaño

Karis Rietema

Sevie Roddy

Anjali Sardar

Avery Saylor

Megan Stevens

Miriam Wieringa

Marcie Woods

Printed in the United States by Chapbook Press.

Table of Contents

Foreword

By Caitlin Horrocks

Like probably many of the people reading this, I was a kid who loved stories. I read much later into the night than my parents realized, and raced through worksheets as quickly as possible so I could pull a book out of my desk. If there was a creative option for homework, I took it, rewriting the endings to assigned books so not all the dogs had to die. But I never saw writing as something that I'd be able to do long term. I don't know who I thought wrote all those stories I loved, but I thought of real-life writers like unicorns or yetis—rare and miraculous and living in some forest or mountain range long ago and far away. They surely weren't real people, not the sort of person I could actually become. I thought of my writing as a waystation on the journey to wherever else my life would lead.

This was only one of my strange, deeply unhelpful ideas about what it meant to be a "real" writer, and how I wouldn't ever be one. I assumed I'd eventually have to set writing aside, but time went by and I just... didn't. I kept signing up for classes, kept an eye out for friends I could talk books with, tried and failed to keep journals, and entered my work in a few student contests that I mostly didn't win. I graduated from college and kept writing, even though I no longer had teachers or deadlines or people in my life who cared if I ever wrote again, who would have loved me just as much if I baked bread or wrote code or waited tables instead. I finally acknowledged that writing truly mattered to me, and I wanted to learn how to do it better.

That realization propelled me to graduate school in creative writing, where I had a second epiphany: writers were not, in fact, as rare as yetis.

In my MFA program I was surrounded by them, and most of them were at least semi-regular people. They were the well-published teachers, but they were also my peers, just stretching our wings. We were "real" writers simply by virtue of having not yet stopped writing. We'd managed to stay at our computers or notebooks long enough to get to this point, even while the world around us offered hundreds of reasons to get up and do something, anything, else. Whatever other talents we might have started with, or worried we lacked—talents for lyrical language or exciting plot twists or memorable characters—we'd most crucially fostered or found within ourselves what writer Michael Ventura calls "the talent of the room": the ability to stay alone in a room and write, even when it gets hard and lonely and the noisy world creeps its fingers under the door, inviting us to spend our time in a million other ways.

So, writers ≠ yetis. But I still had lots of other questionable ideas about who counts as a "real" writer, or what being a "real" writer would mean. I believed that "real" writers were supposed to eventually no longer need things like classes or workshops or beta readers. That I should learn to hunt down problem spots and fix them on my own. And it's true now that when I feel a story isn't living up to whatever spark I was originally trying to capture, I have a much bigger and deeper toolbox of tools to close the gap between concept and execution. But like every "real" writer I know, I can still benefit from talking through a challenge, or having a set of fresh eyes read a draft.

I still benefit from having people to share reading recommendations with, or, let's be real, sometimes literary gossip.

I believed for a while that once I'd revised and polished the first story that I felt really good about, that the next story would inevitably go more smoothly. That writing those stories would teach me how to write a book.

That if an agent agreed to represent that book, that it would surely sell to a publisher, and that if I could sell one, I would sell another. I understood that I had to work hard and write hard. But I thought that that hard work would pay off in clear cut, linear ways: that there would be finish lines on the track, ribbons I could break through and pump my sweaty fists, knowing I'd made it.

That turned out to be pretty much as wrong as the yeti thing.

I learned from watching friends walk their own winding paths that an agent could believe in your book and still fail to sell it. An editor could love your book and then leave their job. A magazine editor could take a story and their magazine could stop publishing fiction. Publishing one book was no guarantee that you'd succeed at publishing, or even finishing, your next one.

While I was watching (or experiencing) such disappointments and detours, I unnecessarily burdened myself with a skewed sense of how little "real" writers should care about such setbacks. I imagined that the truest and best and purest writers wouldn't need commercial success, or even external validation. That I should at least try to grow beyond the need for encouragement. If I was happy with something I'd written, if I'd challenged or pleased myself in some way, I should learn to thrive on that alone. Ideally, I'd someday ascend to a pure state of writerdom in which I could get up every day at 5am and write without even caring whether anyone else ever bought or read or liked it.

I do not get up every day at 5am to write. If I am up at 5am, it is because a child is awake or I have an airplane to catch. I do not write every day. A message from someone who enjoyed my work, or a "yes" from an editor, still give me deep joy and sustenance. I know (and admire) writers who are up every morning cranking out their daily word counts, but I do not know any who exist in a blissful vacuum of Pure Art. They (we) care whether someone reads our words. Not every piece, all the time: there is room in any writer's practice for play, for experiment and failure and yikes and I don't even know what this is but I think I kinda like where it's going.

But of all the various things that I slowly learned don't denote a "real" writer; the real writers I know do hope to communicate with other humans.

Writing is the way we think about and observe the world; we have stories to tell, and we want to tell them in ways that connect with others. We read books, once upon a time, that entertained us and made us feel less alone, and we hope to be able to do that for someone else. In this quest, hungering for "yes's" from editors or judges or teachers or readers isn't a sign that you're a sellout or have a fragile ego, but that writing can be a long road through a dark wood and it's nice to collect those bread crumbs along the way, to tell us that we're on the right path.

I know the metaphor is flawed—the bread crumbs were meant to lead Hansel and Gretel back to where they came from, while the writer is meant to be striking out bravely for somewhere not only they, but no one, has ever gone before. But I wanted to take us to this forest: it's dark and deep, and there are miles to go before we sleep, but if you're there, stumbling over tree roots, you're a "real" writer. If you're looking around, noticing the slant of light through the branches, thinking about the exact right word to describe the crunch of leaves underfoot, congratulations—you're a real writer. If you are reading this anthology, whether in a forest or a comfy chair, and noticing how the writers reeled you in or stuck their landings, if their stories are giving you ideas for your own, you're reading like a real writer. And if you're thinking that that gingerbread house is probably bad news but you decide to explore it anyway so you can write about it later, you are definitely a writer. And you should take your bread crumbs wherever you can find them, and celebrate them, and enlist the people around you to celebrate them, too. For those included in this anthology, seeing their names here in print, I hope this is a delicious bread crumb, one that will sustain you on your forest path.

The poet Li-Young Lee says that when we talk about "the writing life," we actually mean one of two very different things. The first life is the life of scarcity, in which there are a limited number of spots on the bestseller lists, limited space on bookstore shelves, a limited number of pages in anthologies like this. Someone will be in, and someone will be out.

Someone will always be getting something you would have liked to have.

The second writing life is the life of abundance, in which there are more good books than you will ever be able to read in your lifetime, and an infinite amount of joy and sadness and wisdom and laughter available to you in their pages; there are so many fellow writers and readers out there to meet and befriend, either in person or on the page; and there are no limits to what you yourself may someday create.

This anthology, as all anthologies do, contains a limited number of pages and a limited number of stories by a limited number of contributors.

It has one inevitable foot in the life of scarcity. But it stands with its other foot in the writing life of abundance; it was made by and for writers and readers spread across an entire state, eager to hear what stories we have to offer to each other, eager to see how writers at different ages and speaking different languages can speak to each other, and eager to read the literal thousands of pages of humor and heartbreak coming from writers brave and hard-working enough to tell and share their stories.

The writing life of scarcity can fuel you, for a while, either to improve your art or to put yourself out there in sometimes scary ways. But it will also, eventually, make you jealous and sad and unsatisfied. Let's all recognize each other for the real writers we are, who can sit alone in a room and then leave it and listen, really listen, to each other. Let's try to live together the writing life of abundance, and celebrate each other's voices in this noisy, noisy world.

About the Author

Caitlin Horrocks is author of the story collections *Life Among the Terranauts* and *This is Not Your City*, both *New York Times Book Review* Editor's Choice titles. Her novel *The Vexations* was named one of the 10 best books of 2019 by the *Wall Street Journal*. Her stories and essays appear in *The New Yorker, The Best American Short Stories, The PEN/O. Henry Prize Stories, The Pushcart Prize, The Paris Review,* and elsewhere. She lives with her family in Grand Rapids, Michigan, where she teaches at Grand Valley State University.

Adult Judges' Choice Winner

Carrion Crow
Megan Stevens

The house on Evergreen Way looked as if she'd never left, unchanged in the three years since Jerry had last been home. The fan in the upstairs crawlspace was still running. The rose bush under the window was still tall enough to tap on the glass with the faintest breeze. The rusted Bronco in the driveway still looked like it was going to fall to pieces at any moment. The only thing that seemed to have changed was the noise—as she let herself in the front door, the silence was as blaring as the television had been all those years ago.

She found Irina sitting in the living room, surrounded by boxes and boxes of papers and records and folders that Jerry couldn't identify. Irina, too, looked fairly untouched. Not a single curl looked out of place, and she still wore shoulder pads that would have made football players look on her with envy. The only indication that anything had changed was the dark bags under her eyes. She looked... tired. She looked down at the folder open on her lap and looked exhausted.

"Hi," Jerry said, and her mother jumped. Papers scattered everywhere.

"Jesus, Marjorie." Her mother sank back into the couch, a hand pressed to her chest. "You scared me."

"Sorry." Her hip popped as she crouched down to gather the papers off the ancient shag carpet, but at least she was able to stand again. She ruffled the papers a little. The tiny print made her eyes glaze over. "What are you doing?"

"Life insurance." Irina snatched the papers back. "You know how it is," she said, though they both knew that she didn't. "Where are the girls?"

"...college?"

Irina frowned. "You know what I mean."

"They're busy, Mom. They'll be here when we've got a date for the service." Despite every instinct in her body screaming at her to run, she looked around for a place to sit. Every surface was covered with boxes and papers—every surface except the lift chair, which was still partially raised.

She carefully lowered herself onto the edge of the coffee table.

Irina stared at her, huffed, and looked back to her paper.

Jerry sighed. "Please don't."

"I haven't said a word, Marjorie."

Perhaps not, but Irina had never needed words to get her point across.

"As long as you're here, you should go through everything in the guest room. See what you want to keep. Anything you or the girls don't want, I'm tossing."

That was no exaggeration, Jerry knew. She'd barely been out of the house a month before Irina had cleared out her room and turned it into a zen corner.

The door to the guest room stood open, and Jerry stopped for a moment in the doorway to take it all in. Where the guest room usually resembled a quaint inn, it now looked like a music supply store had exploded.

Haphazard stacks of records stood on the dresser, and the bedspread had all but disappeared under a half dozen instrument cases. A dusty old mason jar filled with dulcimer hammers sat on the windowsill. It was a mess that screamed Philip, a mess that would soon be gone, never to be seen again.

She picked her way around the boxes on the floor and traced her fingers over the cracked leather of the violin case that perched on the edge of the bed. Beside it lay the wooden zither case, the two dulcimers, and beside that...

A grin crept across her face as she picked the trombone case out of the pile. She would never have guessed that the trombone was still here—in fact, she'd assumed it was thirty years gone. But when she opened it up, there it was: the dull, tarnished brass she remembered so well. The mouthpiece and slide both stuck, but with some ill-advised elbow grease they fit together.

"Let's see how well the old embouchure held up," she said to herself, then lifted the trombone and blew. A shaky tone came out, fading in and out through the noise of blowing, and the vibration tickled her lips. She laughed, and that didn't help. She let the trombone back down and laughed and tried to catch her breath.

"I should have known."

Jerry looked up to find her mother in the doorway, a small smirk on her lips. "What do you mean?"

"Of course you would have to test it." Irina nodded at the trombone. "You just can't help yourself, can you?"

"I come by it naturally," Jerry returned. As she looked, she caught sight of herself in the mirror above the dresser. A fifty-seven-year-old woman with flyaway hair that was almost gone white looked back, red in the face and smiling. It made her laugh harder.

"You can take it," Irina said. "I doubt I'll have much use for that thing."

"I don't need another instrument, Mom." She wrestled the trombone back into its case, then turned her attention to the dresser.

"Records are coming back." Irina nodded at the stacks. "I should get a good price for those."

Privately, Jerry doubted that. The first stack she rifled through held old standbys—Woody Guthrie, the Kingston Trio, Jo Mapes—the kind of record found at every estate sale ever. The second stack was much the same, but as she shifted through the third she caught a glimpse of a familiar picture.

It was a plain record. The sleeve had been white once, but in the last forty years it had yellowed badly. Dark letters across the top announced the music of "The Family Crowe," and below that smaller script listed a half-dozen songs. Then came the photograph of the family.

It was Philip, young and strong and standing tall, holding the bass fiddle that was long since sold. It was Irina, young and elegant with raven hair, seated at her harp dulcimer. And it was Jerry and Jenny, unsmiling, perfect mirrors from their straight dark hair to the zithers they each held on their laps.

She'd forgotten how similar they'd looked, but of course they had. Twins were supposed to look alike.

"You're getting rid of this?" she asked.

Irina looked it over, her face an unreadable mask. "We haven't had a record player in twenty years. There's no point in hanging onto it."

"But it's..." She couldn't put it into words. "...it's us."

"Do you want it? Take it."

She had a copy somewhere, but that wasn't the point. "It just seems like throwing out the family." Irina shrugged. "That family doesn't exist anymore, now, does it?"

Jerry looked down at Jenny's pale face, white as the lace on the collar of her black dress. She ran a finger over the image of her sister. Jenny had hated that dress. Itchy, she'd said, and too fiddly. Their mother'd had to wrestle her into it.

"Jenny might want it," she said quietly.

Irina turned sharply away. As she stalked back down the hall, Jerry noticed for the first time that she shuffled a little, stooped over like she was searching for a lost needle in the carpet.

Jerry stuck the record back into the pile. Why shouldn't she talk about Jenny? She was a grown woman, and if she wanted to talk about her missing sister, then she'd do it.

She found Irina in the kitchen, leaning against the island and sipping lukewarm coffee. Her mother didn't look her way.

"We should get Dad's obituary in one of the bigger papers." Jerry went to the cupboard for her old favorite glass—a repurposed jam jar. "So she might see it and know, at least." When she glanced back Irina was giving her a very wry, cynical look—the sort of look that said Jerry was being an idiot. Jerry swallowed hard and pressed on. "I know how you feel about it, but if she is out there…"

"If she was still out there, she'd have come home by now. She couldn't manage on her own for a week, let alone thirty years."

"Mom…"

"I don't want to talk about it." Irina cut her off with a sharp chopping motion. "She made her decision a long time ago. We've made ours."

The house was so silent that Jerry could still hear the attic fan whirring away as if it would never stop.

"How are the girls." It wasn't a question.

Jerry took a deep breath and tucked the image of Jenny, unsmiling and unhappy, back into the recesses of her mind. "They're good."

"They write regularly?"

The idea of the twins writing anything at all, let alone letters to their mom, made her smile. "Nobody writes letters anymore. Emily calls me every Wednesday. Sometimes Kara texts me things I don't understand."

Her mother smirked. "And now you know what it was like to raise you."

"And Jenny."

With a sigh, Irina dumped the rest of her coffee into the sink. "Jenny was on a whole different level. It was like raising an alien." Before Jerry could interject she added, "We listened to your record. Your father liked it a lot."

"That's… good."

"I think it was the last album he listened to."

Jerry went to the fridge and pushed through the nutrient shakes and cottage cheese until she found something resembling a beverage. She poured out a bit and took a sip—orange juice?

"I liked it too, of course. The only thing was the title."

"What was wrong with the title?" Jerry had thought it rather clever.

"Carrion Crow" was the first track on the album, so "Carrion Crowe" seemed a fitting title.

"It's just so morbid." Irina shuddered.

"It's a morbid song," Jerry said, and she sang the last verse.

> The old sow died and the bells did toll, Derry derry derry dayo,
> The old sow died and the bells did toll,
> The little pigs prayed for the old sow's soul.

"But still. A title should be something nicer."

Jerry shrugged. It occurred to her that Jenny would have liked the song.

Jenny's favorite songs were always the bleakest, the ones that cleaved the closest to life. While she couldn't remember "Carrion Crow" ever coming up during their youth, she was sure that the song of a tailor trying to shoot a crow from a nearby tree and shooting his own sow instead was one she would have found fascinating.

Something else occurred to her. "Where are Jenny's records, anyway? I didn't see any of hers."

"Oh, I tossed those years ago. It's no wonder she was so miserable all the time. All those angry records. A whole stack of those Phil Pines!"

For a moment, Jerry's mind went blank. "Ochs, Mom. I think you mean Phil Ochs."

"I should have thrown those out long before she left." Irina's posture fell even more. "You know he killed himself? It must have given her ideas. And some of those covers. I'll never forget the one. That awful gold lamé suit. I thought she was listening to..." She dropped her voice and hissed, "Elvis."

"God forbid."

"You laugh, but in my day it was shameful to let your child listen to that rubbish."

"I think Emily used to have an Elvis CD. She thought he was boring."

Her mother sighed and pinched the bridge of her nose.

"That's life, Mom. Tastes change."

"At least you turned out alright. Dad and I got out the CD player to listen to your last album. He... we both enjoyed it a lot. You'll be glad to know he liked your 'Carrion Crow' cover." If she slouched any more Jerry was sure she'd fall to the floor. "I suppose he had an idea what was coming. It made him morbid. But your 'Jaybird' was nice. I always said you were at your best on the harp dulcimer."

"Mmhm." Harp dulcimer had always been Irina's instrument, and neither Jerry nor Jenny had ever been trained in it. Not for the first time, Jerry found herself wondering if Jenny had picked it up in the years after she left. She'd been able to play almost anything she picked up; who knew what she could have learned in thirty years?

"What's next? Are you finally going to do that gospel album I requested?"

Jerry's lips tightened into a smile, and she said, "Emily had an idea I thought sounded interesting—a collection of murder ballads. You know, 'Delia's Gone,' 'Frankie and Johnny,' 'Tom Dooley,' 'Banks of the Ohio.' That sort of thing."

Her mother raised her eyes to meet Jerry's, but her expression was resigned. For a long moment she was silent.

"Sometimes," she said at last, "I think you're as bad as she was."

She walked away, back to the living room, and left Jerry to sip her orange juice in silence.

As she turned to watch her mother go Jerry caught sight of herself in the stove's backsplash, distorted in the aluminum. Once again, she wondered what Jenny would look like in her sixties. Probably not unlike her sister, but Jerry imagined her with her own snowy white hair cut close, grim determination on her face no matter what she was doing, dressed in the plain clothes she always preferred. For some reason Jerry liked to imagine her with the same thick, plastic-framed glasses and cheap suspenders Philip had worn before his death. The image made her laugh.

She took another sip of orange juice before dumping the rest in the sink—neither she nor Jenny had ever been able to stand pulp in their juice—and heading back to the bedroom, carefully avoiding eye contact with Irina as she passed the living room.

Jerry pushed aside the zither case with the chipped handle and took a seat on the bed. From there she could just reach to sort through the records.

A quick shuffle through showed her the usual suspects— the Guthries and Mapeses—and also a Bob Dylan that had somehow survived Irina's purges. Then there was the signed copy of "American Folk Songs for Children." And then she came upon it again—"The Family Crowe."

She paused again, looking down at Jenny, and tried to listen in her memories for the sound of her playing. What came to mind was her sister, nineteen, sitting on the bed with Jerry's trombone and sliding her way through Phil Ochs' "That's What I Want to Hear," struggling to make a sound around the biggest grin Jerry'd ever seen on her face.

Jerry swallowed hard and smiled at the picture, and the picture didn't smile back. She let go of one edge to wipe at her eyes, and it slipped from her grasp. As it fell the record began to slip out. She grabbed for it and barely caught the edge as the cover slipped away, and she found herself face-to-face with a record that definitely wasn't "The Family Crowe." "Greatest Hits," it read. "Phil Ochs."

"Huh," Jerry said to herself. She thought of Jenny as a little girl, never putting the right record back in the right album. But then she thought of Irina's frown as she looked at some of their old records, and she pictured Jenny slipping a "bad" album into a "good" sleeve. She dug her phone from her pocket and snapped a picture of the album, then opened a text chat.

Kara, she typed, can you send me the cover to this album? Love mom

None of the titles sounded familiar—"Chords of Fame," "Ten Cents a

Coup," "No More Songs." Jerry wished like hell she had a record player to be sure, though. She wanted to hear the songs even if she hadn't heard them before, and for some reason it struck her that it would be like listening to an album one last time with Jenny, the way they used to do as teenagers before Jerry moved out.

She didn't try to stop the tears after that thought.

It wasn't logical in any way, which would have annoyed Jenny, but there was something about Phil Ochs that was forever tied with her sister in Jerry's mind. Maybe it was their nature—serious old souls in a young person's body, unable to be still, constantly strumming nervously, taking careful note of every injustice in the world. Maybe it was something else—the way that, in hindsight, they both seemed to be a tragedy waiting to happen.

"Please," Jerry whispered to no one at all, her thoughts on Phil Ochs. Thirty-five years old, he'd been, when he hung himself in his sister's bathroom. "Don't let her have gone like that."

She wanted to say that Jenny wouldn't have. She wanted to believe that when Jenny left their parents' house she went out into the world and built a life of her own in a place where people treasured her the way she deserved to be treasured. With no answers, no evidence at all once she walked out of this house, why not believe the best? Yet Jerry couldn't shake the feeling that she was long, long gone.

In her hand her phone buzzed. Through teary eyes she read Kara's reply.

lmfao

What did that mean, she wondered, but as she did a file began to download. The image she recognized, even if she didn't recognize anything else. There was no mistaking the man standing before the red stage curtains, guitar clutched in his hands, covered from head to toe in gold lamé.

This guy has great taste, Kara texted her. Campy af. Love it.

Jerry laughed, blinking away the tears that stung at her eyes. Yes, she texted back. Jenny'd had a very particular taste, and the nieces she'd never met did too. Jenny would be pleased, she thought. Pleased and proud.

Upstairs, the crawlspace fan ran without stopping. Outside, the rosebush tapped on the window. And in the guest bedroom, surrounded by music, Jerry smiled to herself and hummed aloud. That's what I want to hear.

About the Author

Megan Stevens is a secretary in a university English department. When not writing, she enjoys reading, knitting, and other grandmotherly hobbies. She's not actually a grandmother.

Adult Judges' Choice Runner-Up

I Won't Let This Build up Inside of Me
Chris Cochran

We cross the street and I'm intoxicated.

One hand grips hers; the other, an unopened bottle of wine we've snuck off with from the wedding reception. Mason jar lights flicker in the distance.

The reckless abandonment of inhibition from the dance floor—a faint, buried bass line.

My uneven canter stamps the soil still soft from this morning's rain as we make our way across an unlit field used for overflow parking.

"It's definitely the next row," I insist before hearing a chirp in the opposite direction.

"You sure about that?" Rae flashes a flirtatious smile, having just used the fob to locate her car like a sensible person.

I tuck the wine bottle under my arm, dangerously, in order to hold both her hands.

"You know that—" The wine bottle slips and I instinctually try to catch it with my foot, punting it a short distance instead.

Rae is quite amused with my drunkenness, laughing as she turns around to pick up the bottle of wine. "Still intact! For a second, I thought you ruined everything," she jokes, handing me the bottle. I stifle any professions of love, fearing she's right.

My passenger seat stupor is interrupted by canopy lighting brighter than the sun as we pull to a stop at a Shell station. Against Rae's protests, I pump the gas; chivalry trumps inebriation when you're in love. A small gesture to show her what I can not tell her.

Rae heads inside and I'm looking for a place to swipe my credit card, oblivious to the new chip reader that's been installed, when a gold Honda Accord rolls up beside me. It's a decades-old model in pristine condition.

The driver steps out and leers at me from over the top of her car, her close-cropped red hair ablaze under the gas station lighting. Her large, square glasses rest precariously on her button nose, one shake of the head away from toppling over. She's wearing a denim skirt belted at the waist. A stack of books adorns her plaid top with the letters "A-B-C" forming an arch above.

"It's a chip reader, honey. Do you need me to show you how it works?"

I roll my eyes and insert my card, turning away from Mrs. Deprecor, my first grade teacher. I can feel her eyes boring a hole in the back of my head.

She says, "I was just trying to help, no reason to be—"

"Would you just leave me the hell alone?"

I may have kissed a girl named Marcy in first grade during recess. I suspect she propagated the rumor herself, however, having no memory of the kiss.

Nevertheless, the school was inundated with news of our alleged affair.

Mrs. Deprecor took me aside for interrogation as our class returned from the playground. Kiss or no kiss, I was scared shitless.

She leaned over, hands resting on her knees, and delivered a look of incredulity: "Did you kiss Marcy during recess?"

"I don't know," I said.

"You don't know?"

"Yes."

"Yes, you kissed Marcy?"

"No. Yes, I don't know if I did."

I didn't learn about "Pleading the Fifth" until high school. Mrs. Deprecor stood up, sighed heavily, and decided on a different approach.

"Look, you are not allowed to kiss girls. Do you understand?"

"Like, ever?"

"Not on my watch. Go have a seat."

I hurried away, more confused than before.

Like most first grade teachers, Mrs. Deprecor was relegated to the inner recesses of my brain, a memory that only resurfaced as an occasional answer to a security question for an online account. So when I saw her reflection in a dance studio wall of mirrors at a community college fifteen years later, it was surprising. I was watching a classmate interpretively dance to "Vermillion" by Slipknot for an English class project. This was not surprising and only sounds so to those unfamiliar with community college.

For over five minutes, our class watched a horror movie unfold. If memory serves me correctly, she began her dance by writhing out of television static.

As singer Corey Taylor growled, this talented demon conjured spirits through a slow, disturbingly seductive crawl across the vinyl flooring. Every guy watched a reflection of the performance in the dance studio mirrors, fearful of looking straight into her eyes and either being cast into the underworld or, worse, aroused.

Perhaps I watched the performance a little too attentively—a fact made evident by the reflection of my scowling girlfriend. Our eye contact was a different kind of horror movie altogether.

With traps laid all around, my eyes desperately sought refuge; instead, they spotted Mrs. Deprecor. She was standing amongst the reflection of students at the crowd's edge. She shook her head disdainfully, her glasses slipping down her nose. A colorful arch of letters began and ended just above her crossed arms. She hadn't aged a day since first grade.

I looked away from the wall of mirrors to see the source of the reflection without luck. When I looked back, her reflection was gone.

Leaving campus that evening, I spotted Mrs. Deprecor sitting on a bench in the commons. She looked exactly as I had remembered, her crimson hair not showing the slightest hint of gray—an impressive feat for someone who should have been well into her seventies.

As I approached, she was carefully applying glue to the back of a heart she had cut out of pink construction paper. She began pasting the heart onto red cardstock paper, then looked up to meet my perplexed gaze.

"It's getting chilly. Did you forget to bring a jacket to school today?" she asked as she continued her project, interrupting my rumination.

"What is this? Are you—"

"Have a seat." After confirming no one was in our general vicinity, I sat down beside her, still acknowledging her authority all these years later.

"Sit up straight, you're slouching."

"Why are you here?"

She grabbed a pair of scissors and started cutting a larger heart around the one that she had just pasted. "Your guess is as good as mine. Which makes a lot of sense, when you think about it."

I slowly slid my hands down my face, pushing my closed eyelids with my fingertips, and let out a long sigh.

"My eyes wandered a bit. So what?"

"They didn't use to." She finished cutting out the heart and held it up to admire before reaching over and throwing it in the trash can beside the bench.

"Well that was...not subtle." I watched as Mrs. Deprecor gathered her crafting supplies into a giant satchel, stood up, slung the bag over her shoulder, and walked away.

I spent the following two years trying to fix a hopeless relationship, unwilling to accept the notion that sometimes people just grow apart.

Although never in the same location, I could always anticipate Mrs. Deprecor's arrival when feelings of self-doubt and vulnerability crept in. Her visits were sporadic at first; however, as my relationship neared its end, she appeared often and we settled into a comfortable routine. Our conversations felt like free therapy, which explains why I initially mistook her intentions as helpful rather than sinister.

She would ask me to pinpoint exactly when things went wrong, to consider what I might have done differently. The relationship was framed in a way that suggested mending was possible, that things could get back to what they once were—I just had to fix it.

I had just clicked send on a regretful text to my now ex-girlfriend because the internet told me she was in a relationship but that had to be a mistake because how could she be in a relationship since we were just in a relationship that ended like yesterday and didn't what we have mean anything?

I have no doubt my concerns were elegantly communicated in a respectful and rational manner.

"I told you not to look!" My new roommate. She had moved out, and he had moved in. No time to mourn in private when rent is due.

They had met once, my roommate and ex-girlfriend. She came by a week after we split to pick up the last of her things. When she left, his only comment was that "she smelled like dead flowers." These words were the on-ramp for my long road to recovery.

He was right of course. About her perfume and about avoiding social media.

I was staring vacantly out the window of my second-story apartment, which sat above a grocery store, perhaps looking for a way to escape the mortification I felt after transforming into the type of crazy that only heartbreak can evoke. Mrs. Deprecor was loading groceries into the back of her Honda. We locked eyes for a moment; she shook her head, almost apologetically, closed the trunk, and drove away.

What purpose had Mrs. Deprecor served? Was she trying to help or was she simply delaying the inevitable? For the first time, a splash of bitterness washed over me.

My ex-girlfriend had the decency to never respond to my text and my roommate had the decency to take me on as a third wheel most weekends and time had the decency to drag me along, but Mrs. Deprecor was not as accommodating. Eventually, I began dating again and she was there every step of the way, reminding me that everything I had ever done in the presence of women was bad and that I should feel bad.

"Applebees for a first date?" Mrs. Deprecor slid into the booth that had just been occupied by someone I had allowed my mother to set me up with. "How do you expect any woman to take you seriously when you order mozzarella sticks?"

I looked over my shoulder to make sure my date was not on her way back before whisper-shouting, "Are you crazy? You can't be here—she could return any minute!"

"Honey, she took her purse and coat with her to the restroom. She's not coming back." She was right and seemed smug and satisfied delivering this revelation. "Why did you keep talking about that time you dunked a basketball?"

"I don't know, I was nervous. But it is kind of a big deal. I'm not even—"

"It's not a big deal, and she didn't care."

"There was a lull in the conversation. I had to say something. Besides, I'm not even six feet tall. And look at how short my arms are," I said, my voice becoming more animated as I reached toward the ceiling. I noticed a few sidelong glances, so I lowered my arms and the volume of my voice to an almost inaudible hush. "What am I supposed to talk about?"

"Literally anything else."

Our waitress came over with the check and failed to notice the presence of Mrs. Deprecor but definitely noticed the absence of my date.

"She had to leave early. She, uh, works a night shift," I explained for some ungodly reason. What was wrong with me?

I handed her my card and waited until she was far enough away before turning my attention back to Mrs. Deprecor.

"Can I ask you a question?"

"May you ask me a question."

"Why am I so bad at this?"

"Beats me," she replied. "From what I remember, you were quite the adonis at recess. Of course, you were a mumbling idiot back then, too."

"Well, thanks. This has been helpful."

The waitress dropped off my card mid-stride and continued walking toward another table. I signed my name quickly and stood up to leave. As I was walking away, Mrs. Deprecor called out, "That's your signature? I can't even make out any of the letters. Did they not teach you cursive in third grade?"

It was an early morning after a late night. I watched a scattered fog wind its way around saggy clotheslines and broken lawn furniture from my kitchen window. Through the haze, I noticed Mrs. Deprecor sitting on an old, rusty swing in the abandoned playground across the street from the double-wide that myself and two friends squeezed into shortly after college. I walked over begrudgingly, having at this point already learned the futility of avoidance.

Better just to confront her, get it over with.

"You were out late last night," she said as I sat down in the much lower swing beside her. "Remember our talk about the importance of routine?"

"What do you want?" I asked curtly, but I knew. I always knew.

She stopped swinging, looked down at me, and said in an accusatory tone, "You kissed a girl here last night." I followed her eyes as she looked over at the trailer that was in the lot diagonal to our own, and then I looked down at my feet as they scraped the dirt that had been gouged away beneath my swing.

"Technically, she kissed—"

"Do you really think it wise to start a relationship with a girl who still lives with her ex-boyfriend?"

"Well, it doesn't sound great when you say it out loud," I admitted with a short laugh. "Look, this isn't what you think. I'm not going to feel guilty—"

"And yet, here I am." Mrs. Deprecor jumped off her swing and adjusted her denim skirt. She surveyed our surroundings and shook her head. "Just look at this place," she said in disgust before disappearing into the morning mist.

My first few steps exuded confidence, but then my lower body turned to lead. My friends noticed the hesitation which confirmed what they already knew: There was no way I was going to go through with this. Their playful jeering, however, was enough motivation to keep me trudging along.

She looked up from her drink and we made eye contact as I approached.

This was it—the point of no return. Why were my only two choices dying alone or experiencing extreme discomfort and rejection?

I hadn't even considered what I was going to say, but it ultimately didn't matter. Mrs. Deprecor was lurking at a table in the back corner. She shook her head, reminding me that my actions were both unwanted and inappropriate.

So I mumbled an awkward apology to this poor woman as I walked right past her and straight to the restroom, my friend's laughter in the background playing me off the stage.

"Well, that was embarrassing," Mrs. Deprecor said as she started to awkwardly lift her denim skirt at the urinal beside me.

"Jesus, what are you—" I looked over, regretfully, in an attempt to understand the logistics of what was happening.

My eyes quickly redirected to the wall above my own urinal.

"You really shouldn't be in here." I zipped up and stepped toward the grimy sink, managing to get a modicum of soap from the dispenser after mashing the button several times. As I rinsed my hands under the warm water, I heard Mrs. Deprecor from behind me.

"Have you ever considered just giving up? How do you expect to make someone happy when you're so miserable?"

I looked up and stared at her reflection in the mirror. While her vitriol was meant to harm, it actually had an inverse effect; for the first time, Mrs. Deprecor had actually passed along sound advice.

So I gave up.

That is, of course, until I discovered happiness on my own. And then I met Rae.

I fumble with the gas tank cap until it finally spins off. I shove the nozzle inside, enraged. Mrs. Deprecor begins her belittlement.

"That is not how you talk to an adult." I'm suddenly six again, running up the concrete walkway to get in line at the end of recess. Being pulled aside for a private scolding.

I close my eyes and let her rancor fade into a muffled hum but can only fend it off momentarily. Her words emerge a cacophony of self-inflicted criticism.

"You would have told her by now if you were so sure she'd say it back," she hisses. Enough is enough.

"Why didn't you pull Marcy aside and ask her if she kissed me?" Mrs. Deprecor scoffs and turns away.

"Please don't tell me you're still thinking about—"

"We didn't even kiss! I mean, we probably didn't. We might have. Either way, it's beside the point." I'm rambling, but I refuse to let my drunkenness interfere with this sudden moment of clarity. "I blamed myself because you blamed me."

I stop and take a few breaths, letting the anger subside. "My whole life you've been a constant reminder of how bad I am at all this. Never here to help, just here to criticize."

I notice a subtle shift in her expression—not quite remorse but a lesser hostility.

"You've made it impossible for me to believe that anyone could ever love me. But, of course, you're me. So what does that mean?" I say.

Mrs. Deprecor puts her pump nozzle back in its holder and, for once, is rendered speechless. She huffs angrily, climbs into her car, and quickly pulls away. I watch her taillights shrink into the evening until the clicking of my gas pump brings me back to reality. I turn back to the pump and notice Rae approaching.

"Here you go, drunkie," she says as she holds a literal gallon of water out in front of her with both hands, pretending the weight is almost too much to bear.

"I love you, Rae."

"Are you serious?" she asks. "You're telling me this now? If I would have known a jug of water was all it took, we could have gotten past this months ago." "Ugh, I'm sorry."

"No. God, no. That was not—" Rae looks horrified. "Sorry, tell me again. Do over."

"What?"

"Say it again!"

"I love you!" I blurt out again, saying now twice in ten seconds what I've been unable to say over the past eight months.

"I know," she replies. "I love you, too." We kiss. I'm sure of it.

About the Author

Chris Cochran was born and raised in Berrien County, MI, and currently resides in Stevensville, MI, with his wife and son. He has taught English to high school students for the past decade after obtaining his teaching degree from Grand Valley State University. He enjoys writing coming of age stories.

Adult Readers' Choice Winner

The Walk of Honor
Marcie Woods

It was warm enough to have the window over the sink open on this mid-May Friday evening. Walter Senior appreciated the little breeze that was dissipating the cooking odor. He had gone to the bother of pan frying the franks before adding the beans. Odd that Walter Junior hadn't said anything about dinner. Normally, young Walter was as polite a thirteen-year-old as they came, but something sure seemed to be eating at him tonight. Junior was frowning as he washed the dinner dishes, oblivious to the gust ruffling his hair.

Walter Senior sipped his coffee and studied his grandson's hunched posture. He had taken in the boy four years earlier, after his son and daughter-in-law died in a winter car crash. There was no money left after the funerals, and he and Junior were living on Social Security, but they managed. Walter was a great kid. He did his schoolwork, a good bit of the housework, and never complained about living in his grandpa's tiny place.

This hangdog look was new, and Senior didn't like it. The seventy-five year old finished his coffee and cleared his throat. "Word down at the park is that your school's going to hold a regular walk-the-stage eighth grade graduation."

The fry pan smacked the water in the sink. "They might be holding one, but it doesn't make a difference to me, Gramps. I'm not going to graduation."

"Oh? Now, here I was looking forward to going to it. Looked up the bus schedule and everything."

Walter set his shoulders. He kept cleaning pans with his back to his grandfather. "Sorry to disappoint you, but I am not going."

"Seems to me this is something we need to discuss." Senior pushed his wheelchair away from the table and brought the mug over to the sink. "Why don't you want to go?"

Walter turned on the hot water tap and rinsed the coffee mug instead of answering.

When he reached for other dishes, Walter Senior said, "Junior, those are clean. You're done here, son." He rolled back to the table, and said calmly,

"Why don't you want to go to your own graduation? Last report I got, you were doing fine."

"I'm just not going!" Junior slapped down the dish cloth and stormed out of the kitchen. Senior heard a door slam.

Dammit, I don't need this teenage crap already. Senior muttered a few choice words to himself, picked up the dish cloth, and wiped out the sink.

Then sighing deeply, he rolled down the hall and opened his grandson's door.

Walter was lying on his bed with an arm over his eyes. "Hey!"

"You behaved better when you were nine. In my house, you earn your privileges, you know that. Remember the family motto, son." Senior eased his chair over the threshold. "Now, sit up and talk to me."

At this Walter reared up. "I don't want to go to some stupid, meaningless ceremony. That's all. It's a stupid waste of time."

"That's it? You don't want to do meaningless things? Ha!" snorted Senior.

He wheeled himself up toe to footrest with Walter. "What do you think adult life is, son? It's showing up, doing what you're paid to do, and going home. Over and over, rinse, repeat for fifty years—if you're lucky. You find your own meaning, Junior. It does not come with the job."

"Yeah, well, I don't find any meaning to walking across a stage and shaking my principal's hand. What good will it do?" He glared at his grandfather. "A piece of paper that says I completed eighth grade won't make any difference to my life."

His grandfather glared right back at him. "Don't be so sure of that, kid.

Things happen. My dad died when I was nine, too. Mom tried, but I had to leave school to watch my brother. I finally took a factory job at fourteen.

If I had stayed in school even to the end of eighth grade, I could have had a better job, made more money. I'd have given anything to have a piece of paper like the one you're being offered."

Walter Junior looked surprised. "I didn't know you had to quit school and go to work, Gramps."

"It's life. You do what you have to for family. Remember our motto. But that's why it is important to me that you get that certificate. And I have now run out of patience. I have asked, I have offered discussion -- now I am telling you. There is no way I am allowing you to skip this graduation ceremony. You are going if I have to tie you to a skateboard and drag you behind me! I am going to be in that auditorium, Junior. I want to see with my own eyes that you won't have to settle for menial labor jobs all your life."

Walter stood up and ran his hands through his hair. "There's still a problem, Gramps. I really can't go!"

Gramps leaned back in his chair. Finally. "What's the real problem, son?"

Junior turned his back again to his grandfather, unable to face him. "It's a dress-up thing. The principal said this is a solemn occasion and boys have to wear a jacket and tie."

Senior's shoulders drooped as he let his hands fall into his lap. "Ah."

Walter sank back down on his bed. "I'm sorry, Gramps. I don't fit into the suit I wore to the funerals. I can't get the jacket on at all. And I know there's no money for a new one. I didn't want to tell you. I didn't want to make you feel bad."

Gramps coughed, reached for Junior's hand and squeezed it. "I appreciate that. But I might have something you could wear. Follow me."

He rolled out of Junior's space and led him into to his own room, to the closet. "Pull out the covered hanger in the back left," he told Walter.

Puzzled, Junior stepped into the stuffed closet and pushed things aside, emerging a few moments later with a brown garment bag. "This, Gramps?"

"Lay it on the bed, and open it."

Junior unzipped the bag to see the dark green of an old Army uniform, with wide lapels and chest pockets, and brass buttons down the front. A white shirt and black tie hung neatly with it. Most noticeable were the ribboned medals and an impressive triple row of bars pinned over the left pocket of the jacket. "What is this, Gramps?"

"My unit dress uniform from Vietnam. I want to be buried in it. I thought maybe you could wear the jacket and tie for your graduation."

"Wow, Gramps, I'd love to. But I think I'll have to get permission." The boy reached out to touch a bronze disk hanging from a red and green ribbon.

"Tell me about these medals, Gramps?"

The rest of the evening was a history lesson, the kind that brought grandfather and grandson closer to each other.

Next Monday at school early, Walter went to the library to look up some of the medals his grandfather had shown him. Then he looked up the uniform and the weird hat that was in the bottom of the bag. The librarian let him copy the pictures. Before his first hour History class, he asked his teacher, "Mr. Shaffer? When school began, didn't you tell us you were a vet?"

"I'm still in the Army Reserves, and I did a couple tours in the sandbox.

Why?" "Could I talk to you after school? It's about my grandpa. He's a vet."

Mr. Shaffer said sure, and started class, and Walter did some serious thinking.

Graduation was scheduled for the first Friday in June. The week before, there were class parties, end of the year project presentations, and some lucky classes watched movies. What made Walter happiest was the principal's announcement that the High School Parent Teacher Organization was sponsoring a used suit and jacket collection, just as they did prom dresses, and that any student who had outgrown his current suit might exchange it for one that fit. The National Honor Society was running it and would act as clerks to help any eighth graders who showed up. Walter took his too-small suit and discovered a blue blazer that fit, and a cool yellow shirt. He also discovered that a lot of other kids he knew were there, too.

On the night before graduation, Walter Junior watched his grandfather polish his boots and buttons. He wasn't allowed to help, but Gramps said he would need Walter to help him get the boots on. Then he skewered Walter with a no-nonsense look. "You're sure this History teacher said I should wear my rig."

"Yes, sir. We had a big talk about wearing a real uniform and that if we wear it with the medals the original guy had, we'd be, um--"

" 'Stealing his valor.' That means trying to get the glory without doing the work. He sounds like a good teacher, Junior."

Walter was examining the tin of shoe polish like it was very interesting. "Uh, Gramps?"

Gramps raised one bushy eyebrow and grunted, "Yeah? Out with it, kid. You've been twitchy about something for a couple weeks now. 'Bout time you spilled."

Walter twisted the cap on the little Brasso bottle, and his grandfather moved it away from him. "Time's up, son. Whatever you need to say, say it now."

"I asked the principal for special permission, and I got it. I want you to cross the stage with me."

Gramps opened his mouth, shut it, then sat back. "Repeat that."

"When I asked about me wearing your uniform, since that answer was 'No,' I asked if you could accompany me across the stage to get my certificate. You told me to get it for you, Gramps, so I am. And I want you right there with me. The principal didn't have a problem except we will cross at the end instead of in alphabetical order." His grandfather was still looking taken aback, and Walter added, "It's all arranged, Grandpa. Please don't be upset."

Walter Senior put down the shoe he was holding, and the polishing cloth. "I kind of think I'm honored, Junior. Glad at least my jacket still fits."

He looked over at the young man anxiously waiting to see if there was any other reaction.

"And son—that was a nice gesture on your part. I appreciate it. I'll try to do you honor, too."

Walter Junior was nervous. He had arrived early, with the rest of the eighth grade cohort. Mr. Shaffer had promised that someone from his reserves unit would pick up his grandfather in an Ambucab, and bring him to the school, and get him on the right level for the stage. Walter was still nervous, hoping that tonight's action was the right thing to do.

The graduation ceremony was the last part of the evening. Walter sat with the rest of his class in the front of the auditorium while the choir sang, and the school orchestra played. Then, as the orchestra played America the Beautiful as quietly as they could, the students filed into the wings. The principal and several teachers, all wearing academic gowns, stood by a table at mid stage to hand out the certificates. The President of the School Board called out the names, and one by one, smiling bashfully or wobbling on their first high heels, Walter's classmates crossed the stage to applause, the occasional whistle or a cheer. At the far side a photographer snapped pictures of each student shaking the principal's hand or holding up the certificate, before returning, still grinning, to their seats. Walter Junior found his grandfather backstage and carefully took hold of the wheelchair's handles and moved into position at the end of the line.

When Nancy Zywicki beamed for the photographer, the people in the auditorium started to rustle their programs, but stopped as the orchestra went silent; then drumrolls began the flourish that started a soft rendition of The Battle Hymn of the Republic. Mr. Shaffer now stood in his Army Reserve Officer's uniform at the podium. He told the audience that there were two more graduations to celebrate.

"Walter O'Connor, Junior, accompanied by Weapons Sergeant Walter O'Connor, Special Forces, 1964-1967."

Walter nudged the wheelchair, and he and his grandfather moved slowly across a stage that now looked as long as a football field. Gramps sat up at attention, the flash on his Green Beret cocked over his left eye. A ripple of applause broke out in the audience and suddenly everyone on the platform and in the auditorium was clapping. Walter turned his grandfather's wheelchair so he could see the audience. The other old guys Gramps played chess with in the park were there, and all of Walter Senior's friends from the Legion.

Mr. Shaffer held up his hand, and said, "Sergeant O'Connor's commendations from his service include a Purple Heart and a Silver Star.

Tonight we are privileged to extend a lesser certificate, but one he has wanted since forced to quit school in the eighth grade to support his family: a certification of High School graduation, signed by the State Secretary of Education, in acknowledgment of his lifetime contributions of service, demonstrating the qualities of valor and honor." At those words, Senior sat up even higher, and Junior's eyes opened wide.

Then Mr. Shaffer added, "And, Walter Junior, here is your certification of graduation from the eighth grade." Junior shook Mr. Shaffer's hand and took the certificates. Gramps snapped a salute and Mr. Shaffer returned it. Everyone on stage and in the auditorium was on their feet, applauding.

The photographer was taking picture after picture, but the best one was of Walter Senior with his arms wrapped around his grandson, and both were beaming with accomplishment: Valor and Honor. It was their family motto.

About the Author

Marcie Woods has been a member of Peninsula Writers for about 20 years, and credits their small groups with helping her refine her work. Now retired, she taught literature, composition, grammar, creative writing and college writing courses at the high school and college levels. Marcie was delighted to stop grading student papers but misses the students themselves.

Adult Spanish Lanuage Winner

Tres Mujeres
Sara Proaño

Digamos que las conocía de la forma profunda y misteriosa en la que puede conocer a alguien a la edad de cinco años. O de pronto lo correcto es decir que ellas me conocían a mí. Lo cierto es que como adulta, la imagen de estas tres mujeres siempre ha revoloteado impaciente sobre mi cabeza queriendo ser invaginada y escrita en papel, inmortalizando así su historia.

Tengo que mencionar que no todos los hechos aquí descritos deben considerase fieles a los hechos. Mi memoria tenía cinco años cuando los archivó y a esa edad la imaginación hace parte de la realidad.

Todo aconteció en la casa de la calle Orellana en Quito-Ecuador. Era una casa antigua con ventanales altos y patios extensos cubiertos de jardines, plantas y maleza, y protegidos por una pared de ladrillos de adobe que habían sido pintados con cal por un solo lado, hacía ya muchos años.

La casa había pertenecido al embajador Francés y tenía varias alas que en otros tiempos habían sido elegantes salones y habitaciones que sin duda hospedaron a personalidades del quehacer diplomático de Quito. Los pisos eran de madera pesada, igual que las puertas y hacían sonar cada pingo de la estructura al abrirse y al cerrarse.

En la entrada había varias palmas exóticas y enormes egidas a los lados de la puerta de metal fulgido y que marcaban la entrada y salida de la casona.

Una de las palmas era hogar de un pequeño monito con el que mi hermano y yo nos entreteníamos echándole huevos para que se los comiera muy elegantemente. Se llamaba Martin y nunca dejaba el árbol porque estaba amarrado al él, pero se daba maneras de mover su cadena de arriba a abajo de acuerdo a su estado de ánimo.

Había también un corcel, valiente y diligente que marcaba el paso en medio de las implacables selvas de la parte trasera de la casa y con cuya compañía podíamos aventurarnos sin temor a los lugares más inhóspitos del gran patio. Se llamaba Sanber y era un perro San Bernardo que gentilmente nos permitía montarlo.

JUANITA

La casa había sido dividida en cuatro departamentos de alquiler para así ayudar con los gastos de la propietaria, la señora Juanita. Ella había quedado viuda hacía ya algunos años y teniendo la responsabilidad de criar a su hijo Miguel, se había dado maneras de producir sueltos con la casa. Nosotros vivíamos en el ala izquierda, en un departamento de una sola habitación, cocina y baño que ella había adaptado lo mejor que podía.

Juanita era una dama gentil y sencilla, que ofrecía una sonrisa cada vez que pedía algo y estaba siempre pendiente de nosotros.

Se dice que hace años, cuando todavía era muy joven, servía como empleada doméstica para el señor embajador y su familia. Que era tan eficiente y confiable y que la familia la había adoptado como un miembro más y hasta se la llevaban con ellos cuando salían de vacaciones. Madame Chanaba le enseñó mucho de la comida y cultura francesas: a decir algunas palabras y a comportarse con altura en una reunión social. Está de más decir que sobraron las oportunidades de observar a gente de alta alcurnia mientras se ofrecían fiestas en la gran casa. Todo estaba a su cargo. La cristalería, platería, porcelana china, manteles, listones y la despensa de bienes. Durante estos años ella aprendió a ser indispensable y al mismo tiempo invisible. Los anos pasaron y los hijos de la casa salieron a estudiar en Europa para nunca regresar. Madame Chanaba lentamente fue limitando sus compromisos sociales a causa de una enfermedad de la que no se hablaba y así poco a poco se fueron poniendo en bodega cada candelabro, cristal y porcelana hasta que la casa quedo vacía y oscura.

El embajador llegaba solo para dormir. Se levantaba temprano y volvía a salir a veces sin ni siquiera tomar desayuno.

Una fría mañana, mientras Juanita sacaba a tender las sabanas recién lavadas, escucho a los perros haciendo un ruido extraño del que los viejos hablan allá por la montaña donde ella nació. En seguida sintió como un escalofrió que subía por su espalda y dejando caer la sabana se apresuró a la alcoba de Madame. Era tarde, acababa de morir.

El funeral fue sencillo pero elegante. Exactamente como la exquisita dama le hubiese gustado. Juanita se encargó de casi todo, excepto de dar la bienvenida, porque en ese tiempo, y aun ahora, las empleadas deben ser invisibles.

Entonces sí que pasaron los años. El señor embajador se retiró de su carrera diplomática y decidió quedarse en Quito anticipando que no tendría mucho reconocimiento en su propia tierra si regresaba ahora después de tantos años. Sus hijos no lo visitaban; la casa envejeció con el y también Juanita.

Un día, estando Monsieur Chanaba sentado frente al fuego y mientras observaba a Juanita recorrer la habitación limpiando y acomodando todo su desorden de tercera edad, una idea inquietante se plantó en su mente:

¿Quién se encargaría de el en sus años venideros? ¿Quién le calentaría los pies o le prepararía la comida? Estaba solo y se sentía viejo.

Sabía el que la fiel Juanita tenía derecho a salir de esa lúgubre casa y vivir, que ella no pertenecía al mundo de la vejez y era su responsabilidad soltarla. Pensó con ternura en la dedicación que esta hermosa mujer había demostrado a lo largo de su vida y su corazón se llenó de agradecimiento.

Desde entonces fue aún más gentil y amable con ella, mientras pensaba en dejarla ir con un buen dinero de retiro.

Juanita por su parte no podía consentir la idea de abandonar a su patrón, ella era quien mejor sabía lo que el necesitaba o quería y solo ella podía convencerlo de cualquier cosa.

Puede el lector, en este punto, imaginar toda clase de escenas que seguramente ocurrieron entre estas dos almas, lo cierto es que terminaron casándose y ella le devolvió la vida que el creía haber perdido.

Viajaron, fueron a Europa, visitaron el caribe y una vez más la casa se llenó de vida. Como es de esperarse la gente comentaba toda clase de horrorosas invenciones acerca de esta pareja. "Imagínese, el viejo y ella joven, el educado y ella una bruta..." pero en cada evento que la casa ofrecía, el buen gusto y la distinción eran evidentes. Juanita había aprendido bien.

Años pasaron y Miguelito nació. Ahora sí que la gente hablaba. Hasta entonces todo el mundo imaginaban una inocente relación de mutua conveniencia, pero la verdad era otra. Lo cierto es que el amor es una flor que nace en los más extraños parajes y sobrevive solo cuando ambas partes deciden mantenerla viva.

Eventualmente Monsieur Chanaba murió y dejo todos sus bienes a su señora esposa: Juanita Chanaba. Ella ha cuidado de todo y de todos. Hoy en día es una mujer entrada en años, pero con el rostro dulce a pesar de lo amargo de todo lo que le ha tocado enfrentar. Juanita tiene y entrega vida a donde quiera que va. Su secreto: fe en el amor.

MARUJA

En el centro de la casa y mirando hacia la puerta principal, estaba la puerta de la hermana Marujita. Su figura delgada y oscura permitía identificarla a lo lejos. Siempre vestía de negro, caminaba lentamente y sonreía mientras que nos llamaba con los diminutivos más expresivos que jamás escuche.

No salía con mucha frecuencia, solo a comprar el pan y de vez en cuando a la Iglesia. Vivía sola en una habitación casi vacía y pobremente decorada.

Marujita venia de una familia adinerada de la capital y había sido educada en los mejores colegios de Quito.

Se dice que siendo aún muy joven fue enviada al convento como parte de un voto que su madre había hecho a la Virgen de la Dolorosa. Ella era la hija designada a llevar la carga espiritual de la casa y como tal, tenía que hacerse monja.

En el convento todo era frio y callado, muy diferente a la comodidad y bullicio de la casa paterna. Las largas horas de rezo e instrucción le eran insoportables y aunque trataba, no podía sumergir su mente en las meditaciones de la madrugada.

La madre superiora se percató rápidamente de la falta de espíritu novicial en esta joven y cuestionó con energía su vocación, sin embargo, siendo de la familia Donoso, donantes importantes de la orden de la Dolorosa, no era posible una expulsión.

Se propusieron entonces las hermanas quebrar su espíritu hasta hacerla abrazar el llamado, pero ni castigos, ni amenazas lograron consagrar la mente de Marujita para la vida del convento. De hecho, la conducta cada vez más y cruel de las monjas contrastaba fuertemente con la imagen del Cristo doliente que entrega su vida por todos y la rebeldía hervía por dentro del alma joven de Maria Donoso.

Años pasaron y los barrotes de las ventanas altas del convento fueron reforzados por rumores de que algunas novicias acostumbraban escalar las paredes para ver el mundo de afuera. La separación era tal que ni siquiera noticias de la familia eran permitidas por temor a que el corazón se desvíe. Marujita vivió el duelo de la soledad y el abandono, pago injusto por la salvación de su familia. Con frecuencia era castigada por las más absurdas faltas y debía pasar días en encierro o sufrir la pena del látigo.

Un buen día y mientras miraba las nubes que se movían libres en el cielo azul de Quito, decidió terminar con todo este dolor. Su voluntad había sido quebrantada pero dentro muy adentro sabía que si no escapaba iba a morir en esta celda rodeada solo de piedras y de soledad.

Pensó y pensó por días la mejor manera de salir sin ser vista. Se enteró de las horas de la entrega de remesa y del horario de los fieles. Pensó en cada detalle, planeó su escape con mucho cuidado, pero olvidó algo. Poco sabía ella del profundo dolor que le iba a costar tal decisión. El escape fue relativamente sencillo y una vez afuera tomo el bus de Colon Camal para ir a la casa de sus padres. Al llegar, ya el convento había telefoneado para informar a la familia no solo del escape sino también de la expulsión de Maruja por parte de la madre superiora bajo el cargo de rebeldía e inmoralidad.

Ese día perdió no solamente su afiliación al convento, pero su apellido y su herencia, luego de haber sido humillada públicamente por sus padres a quienes nunca les había tocado vivir vergüenza semejante.

Sin hogar, nombre ni ocupación, salió Maruja de la casa paterna. Sin saber a dónde ir ni donde pasar la noche. Ella sabía que ninguno de los allegados le tendería una mano porque al hacerlo también estarían traicionando la tradición católica y la amistad de familia.

Paso algunos días en un hostal cercano que pagó con los últimos centavos que tenía y luego con algo de dinero que su joven sobrina logro conseguir secretamente.

Mientras más pasaban los días menos esperanza se veía en el futuro de la ex novicia. ¿Separada de la sociedad y de la Iglesia, habría otro lugar en donde encontrar aceptación y ayuda? Por primera vez clamo a Dios en profunda angustia y le pidió socorro y perdón.

Ese mismo día y mientras caminaba por la vereda escucho algunos cantos que salían de una vieja puerta que antes había sido un teatro. Atraída por la música y sin nada más que hacer decidió entrar. Fue así como Juanita y Marujita se conocieron, en esa nueva Iglesia evangélica congregada en un viejo teatro.

Esta demás decir que el departamento de la mitad de la casa no representaba rédito alguno para Juanita, la dueña de la casa y que ambas damas se apoyaban mutuamente medio de una sociedad llena de miedo y prejuicio.

Aun la llaman "la hermana Marujita". Su voz característica es prueba viva de la fidelidad de ese Dios que encarna la fe a través de la práctica de la misericordia y la búsqueda de la verdad.

LUCITA

En el ala derecha y bajo un solar, estaba la puerta azul que daba a la pequeña habitación de la hermana Lucita a la cual nunca entré, no sé si por temor o por respeto. Ella era una dama elegante de cabello blanco siempre recogido hacia atrás, con rostro distinguido. Imponente, casi sin arrugas, alta y esbelta. Usaba botas largas y blusas de seda con cuello de tortuga combinadas con faldas de paño oscuro. Siempre llevaba consigo una cartera, su Biblia y un paraguas porque en Quito nunca se sabe cuándo va a llover.

Pasaba mucho tiempo fuera de casa. A veces en reuniones de la Iglesia, orando por los enfermos o visitando alguna que otra alma.

Quien la viera nunca adivinaría su situación. Lucita, como le gusta que le llamen, nació bonita. Desde pequeña era graciosa y hay quien dice que su padrino era sastre y por eso llevaba con gracia los más caprichosos diseños que la ciudad podía soportar. Como es de esperar, llamaba mucho la atención y más aun cuando, ya en la adolescencia, le costaba esconder sus contornos tan voluptuosos y perfectos.

No sé decirles, por obvias razones, las circunstancias que le llevaron a la escogencia del estilo de vida que llevo antes que yo la conociera y de hecho sé que a ella no le gusta hablar del tema, pero alguna vez mientras leía un libro descubrí la historia de una mujer que había sido tanto el descanso como la pesadilla de cada esposa de la capital y supe que se trataba de ella. Era la prostituta más cotizada de la ciudad. Se dice que su clientela iba desde políticos y negociantes hasta obispos y cardenales; y hay quien asegura que muchas decisiones del gobierno se tomaron informalmente en sus aposentos y bajo sus sábanas.

También supe de rumores que, durante un evento bien documentado alrededor del año 1950, en el que una radio muy popular fue reducida a cenizas a causa de transmitir un radio drama que simulaba una invasión marciana, muchos hombres, convencidos de que el fin del mundo había llegado, confesaron a voz en cuello sus pecados con Lucita.

Lo cierto es que luego de esta catástrofe, muchos más chismes tanto ficticios como reales, resultaron en ruina financiera y sanción social. Su vida de reina se vino abajo por primera vez, y fue allí cuando alzó sus ojos al cielo para encontrar refugio y perdón. Una cadena televisiva de noticias que apenas estaba empezando su transmisión presentó un especial basado en su vida que resultó siendo todo un éxito y grabó el testimonio en el que ella, personalmente, describía su cambio de vida.

De eso ya hace un tiempo y desde entonces mucho se ha dicho de ella y poco se hecho por ella.

La gente olvida los relatos del pasado y muchas veces los protagonistas quedan en silencio. Quisiera poder contarles una historia diferente, pero la verdad es que luego de su conversión pública, fueron muchas dificultades las tuvo que enfrentar: ¿En qué trabajar? ¿Qué hacer ahora? ¿Con quién contar? ¿A quién recurrir en caso de una enfermedad? Es triste reconocer que la comunidad evangélica que tanto se jactó de su cambio de vida, la abandonó en sus últimos años.

Todavía la vemos de vez en cuando porque va a visitar a mi papa a la oficina para pedir alguna ofrenda de amor y dejarle saber cómo se encuentra de la última dolencia que sufre. Siento una profunda compasión por ella, que siempre está dispuesta a dar y a ensenar, a compartir y ofrecer testimonio pero que al mismo tiempo lucha con su propia soledad.

Sigue hermosa, aunque ya anciana, habla fuerte y debo decir en honor a la verdad que está llena de esperanza, Lucita siempre espera que las cosas sean mejores. Ella confía, aun en su soledad, ella sigue confiando. Estas tres mujeres marcaron mi vida. A veces me pregunto, ¿porque tuvieron que vivir tanto dolor y rechazo ellas hermosas mujeres? ¿para qué tanto prejuicio juzgándolas y rebajándolas? Me da rabia reconocer tanta injusticia. Pero puedo pasarme la vida preguntándome y al responder, amargando mi propia existencia como mujer. O puedo, en honor a mi género, contar su historia y con asombro observar su capacidad de resiliencia.

Quiero pensar que es sobre ellas, y tantas más, que hoy tenemos la oportunidad de narrar nuevas historias. De dar fe del trabajo y la sabiduría de las mujeres del aquí y el ahora. Quiero ser yo una de las que forje su propia historia y tambien ser testigo de la tuya, compañera, amiga. Es hora de entender que somos protagonistas y que, aunque no nos demos cuenta, siempre hay ojos que nos están viendo y seguramente serán ellos los que un día contarán esta historia.

About the Author

Sara Proaño has always been fascinated by stories as windows into the souls of their authors. She enjoys listening and communicating through poetry and creates narratives inspired by her multicultural and multilinguistic backgrounds. She is a wife and mother, a professional, a friend and a learner in all forms and stages of life.

Adult Published Finalist

Glint
Emilee Ceuninck

The days when he asks me to join him in the woods are always my favorites.

It's not that I particularly like nature, but I appreciate escaping. Learning. Exploring. And Aman. Especially Aman. He's so...different from everyone else I know. He's soft and knowledgeable. But above all, he's predictable. And I need a little stability in my life. Well, maybe even a lot.

Our little treks through the woods are everything to me, and I would be lost without them. The days when he doesn't ask me to go into the woods are...not good. But let's not dwell on that since today happens to be one of the good days.

"Cass, are you sure you want to come?" Aman asks for the hundredth time, running his fingers through his too-short dark hair. "It's going to be incredibly boring. Again."

"You can't get rid of me that easily," I pout, amused by his standard questioning. He's always pleased that I actually want to go, relishing the agreement every time as if it's the last. We're at our official meeting place—Big Bad Boulder—on the outskirts of the village. Not many people venture into the woods, fearing evil inside. But we have trampled the paths and scoured every cave, and the most frightening thing we've ever found was a pile of abandoned clothes. We never did track down the owner. Or a body. I think Aman ended up giving them to one of his many brothers. Everyone in town admires what gentle, kind people the Greers are.

"I still can't figure out why you come with me," Aman chuckles. "No one else is courageous enough. Besides, you seem more like a city slicker than anything. I would think you'd be appalled by the woods."

"Pish posh," I deny, self-consciously tucking a loose hair from my bob behind my ear. It's somehow a crime here to have stylish hair. The rest of town does not devote much attention to their appearance, further alienating me. But I love short hair too much to compromiseeverything. I've already given up enough.

We wordlessly step into the forest, instantly transported to the sanctuary.

Trees envelop us on every side, the clatter of the forest animals filling our ears. The expanse of pines provides comfort, even here where they are sparse.

Aman and I never talk much during our ventures, sticking to the trail to see what we come across. His purpose here is all business. Aman collects things along the way to sell in the town square; even generic goods that are a dime a dozen out here, like pinecones, fare well. He makes a good living trading, enough so that he is well-respected in town and has his own dwelling at only age twenty-one. I guess it pays to be fearless. And to not have the whole town claim you're completely mad.

Our relationship is simple. I admire all of Aman's qualities, appreciating him from afar. I like watching him in the forest: the gentle way he brushes branches aside, the care in which he handles the items he finds—even the ones that aren't delicate—and mainly the wide smile he throws my direction when the sun is shining just right.

He has very nice hands. So different from the others I've seen; his are the kind made for holding. While every part of him is small and slightly bony, his hands are large and muscled. They appear out of place as if belonging to another. At first, I didn't like them much, being as they were so jarring, but I've grown to appreciate their definition with time. But the thing I love most about Aman is that he doesn't ask a lot of questions. And it's not that he isn't attentive—I can practically see his curiosity leaking through like the rest of town—but he's respectful.

It's almost an unmentioned truth between us. We can wander into the woods together. We can be the friends who occasionally hold hands. But we cannot ask how I got here. Why a random twenty-year-old city gal showed up alone in the forest over a year ago with no story to share. And why she continues to return to it.

"My brother Virgil and his wife are visiting," Aman announces, breaking the accustomed silence. I nod, unsure of why he's sharing. "I think they're expecting."

"You'll be a good uncle," I offer, knowing the importance of family to him.

"I hope so," he replies, clutching my hand in his. It's warm and sweaty. The contact surprises me. Usually, he will only give up the use of his hand on the return of a particularly sorry venture. He guides me in a different direction toward the waterfall.

"But there are no berry bushes this way," I protest. I have this entire forest mentally mapped on the ready. And I know that he does too. Our original ventures included exploring the depths, an alliance formed after continually bumping into each other. I decided he was worth a try. He is safe enough.

"Maybe something's changed," he says, causing a quick relent. He knows I cannot resist ensuring my mental map stays accurate. That irking possibility will get me every time. However, with the grounds incredibly battered, the forest rarely deviates.

He leads the way to our new destination, squeezing my fingers as we cross the small log strewn over the shallows. The water rushes in the distance, splashing us as we carefully balance to safety. He immediately plops down in the small grassy area near the water. I stand next to him, unsure of what to do.

There is no precedent for this behavior.

"Do you not feel well?" I inquire, looking down into his light blue eyes and searching for signs of illness or pain.

"Never better," he replies, his entire face lighting up. "Sit down."

"Why?"

"I've been doing some thinking."

"That's nothing new."

"Just humor me."

"This is highly unusual."

"Please," he whines, his pleading eyes bearing into mine. I know those eyes so well, and they melt me almost instantly.

"Fine," I concede, taking the place next to him. I draw my legs to my chest and wrap my arms around them. Aman doesn't say anything more. I glance around at the familiar waterfall and stream. The water is clear enough to drink and serves as the perfect guide out of the forest. The ground is slightly squishy beneath me, and we get sprayed by the occasional mist of the falling drops. It is my absolute favorite spot in the entire woods. The perfect escape.

I open my mouth to ask why we have stopped here, but I've learned not to ask too many questions if you won't answer any in return. But Aman picks up on my hesitation, replacing it with one of his trademark megawatt grins.

"It's beautiful here," he comments.

"Yes," I agree.

He reaches over and takes my hand in his again, guiding it to his lap. He starts again,

"I've been thinking."

"You've already said that."

"Yes, but this is the way I rehearsed it last night," he laughs. I aimlessly nod, unsure of what he's after. "I've been thinking about...us. What we do. What we are. We fit in some bizarre way. And I'm tired of just loving you from a distance."

"I admire you from afar, too," I admit, despite my better judgment. I promised myself I wouldn't get too close to anyone. Even Aman. But his eyes shine, making my stomach flutter hungrily, and providing confidence in my choice.

"I want to be us outside of the forest," he continues. Outside of the forest? The disapproval gets stuck in my throat. "I love everything you are. I want a chance to learn everything about you."

"You can't love me," I protest. "You barely know me at all!" Despite the year we've spent traveling into the woods together. Exactly the way it must be.

"Only because you won't let me love you properly," he groans. "It's incredibly frustrating. You're so different from everyone else. Your words have more meaning. You understand the importance. Cassandra, you've tantalized my senses. Please let me do the same to you."

"Aman," I start, "I already love you."

"Then nothing stands in our way."

"But I cannot be your lover."

"I assure you it wouldn't be some kind of torrid affair," Aman rushes. "It would be a proper courtship."

"No," I laugh, purposefully averting my gaze. "I'm worried about what the town would say."

It's a simple lie, easier than the truth of why I can't be with him. With anyone. Ever again. "Fleck what they say. That doesn't matter." Even he must realize the town thinks I'm crazy.

"But it does," I argue. "For you."

"I cannot continue this way. It's burning me." His soft expression weakens, his eyes closing.

"I need more time," I offer, willing to do anything to remove the pain while sticking as close to the truth as feasible.

"Are you not alone? Is there someone else?"

"There is no one else," I say through my teeth, running my fingertips over the top of his eyelids. Not anymore. Not for a long time now.

"Then you don't love me?" he questions, slowly fluttering his eyes open.

"You are the only one I trust."

"Do you feel this?" Aman asks, pulling my hand to his beating heart. "This is yours. It is all for you."

"Maybe...slower," I suggest, unable to bear his suffering at my expense any longer.

"What?"

"Maybe I could be yours in the forest to start."

"Really?" he grins, the expression warming me. And it would be nice to explore Aman.

Maybe he really is the hidden reason I come to the forest. Perhaps I am ready.

"But we should get moving," I declare, standing up.

"Okay," he agrees. His smile is contagious. When he gets up beside me, he is almost the exact same height. Everything about him is comforting: mannerisms and size. "Let's pick the golden berries down by the steam." I nod, surprised he'd select somewhere so far away when we've already lost daylight on our detour.

We start down the path. However, this time he places a hand on the small of my back as if to steady me.

"Where do you live?" he asks. I stop, the once gentle hand smacking into my back at the sudden lack of movement.

"Why?" I question, attempting not to sound accusatory.

"I just wasn't sure. I've only ever seen you in town square outside of the forest, and we've always met at Big Bad Boulder. I was thinking maybe I could pick you up next time."

"You don't have to do that," I say, starting back down the trail.

"But I want to," he counters, slipping his hand back into mine. It feels large. I look down, and it appears even bigger than usual. Are his hands still growing?

That seems unlikely. It must be the angle. But for a second, it looked just like...no. This is Aman. Small, safe Aman. No one else.

"We will continue to meet at the rock," I decide, leaving no room for argument.

"What do you do on the days we don't come to the woods?"

"What?" I stammer, feeling my heartbeat quicken.

"Perhaps, if you're free, we could do something non-forest related."

"I said no to being a couple in town," I deflect. He can never know the truth.

"Alright, but I still want to know more about you. Cass, you intrigue me beyond end. What are your hobbies? Do you have a job?"

"It doesn't matter."

"Of course it does. You are important to me."

"It doesn't matter," I repeat, subconsciously picking up the pace as if I can run away from his questions and his breach of trust.

He shuffles to catch up, coming alongside me, "Cass, let me in." I glance at him, hoping not to find him crestfallen. His expression still appears hopeful, but his...nose! Instead of the small button nose perfectly accenting his features, his nose is now monstrous, towering over his mouth. The large nostrils twitch at me, taunting my memories.

"Aman, your nose!" I cry, clutching my own.

"What?" he questions, reaching up. He gives the beast a light squeeze. "It feels alright. Is it bleeding?"

"No. It's...bigger."

"What!?" he reaches up again. "It feels the same as always."

"Are you sure?"

"Positive."

I look at him again and am still met with the same conclusion. Maybe it's the heat? Could it cause some sort of swelling? It must be pretty hot outside today. But I'm out here so often I don't notice it anymore. Or maybe it is some sort of reaction? Perhaps a bad bug bite?

"It's probably nothing," I attempt to reassure him. He finally drops his hand from his nose, which are both still larger than normal.

"Anway, why don't you ever take anything from the forest?" Aman continues as we resume our trek.

"That is not why I am here," I answer honestly.

"But you could still grab stuff and..."

"Aman..." I stress, and he looks away. Why is he doing this to me? Even after I admitted my love?

"This is so difficult," he cries, running his fingers through his hair. I take a second glance and notice he's now...shaggy. His once cropped hair now falls into his eyes. Did he stop cutting it? Did I just not notice? That seems highly unlikely. But the days do seem to meld together.

I let him stew the rest of the way to the bushes, relishing the quiet. The way it is supposed to be. The golden berry bushes are at the very edge of the stream, next to the field. The air is clearer here, despite the trees being denser.

Once we arrive, Aman begins to fill his satchel. I watch wordlessly, every once in a while collecting the smiles he throws my way. I try not to look too closely, not wanting to see him changed. To see someone else. I am just content he no longer appears to be suffering.

After some time, he whispers, "Can I ask you a question?" so quietly I barely hear him. "No," I reply, wishing he'd be my simple, non-questioning Aman again.

"Just the one. I promise not to ask anymore if you answer this one."

"Forever?"

"Forever is a long time," he mumbles, looking down.

"Today?" I twitch from foot to foot.

"Agreed," he smiles. "Why did you come to town?" I feel my throat start to close. My vision blurs, and sweat drips down my arms. I open my mouth to deny, but nothing comes out. It isn't like he's the first to ask. Everyone has. And no one can know. But Aman. Not Aman. He doesn't ask me such things.

"Cass?" he exclaims, dropping his bag at his feet and rushing to me. I look up at him, surprised by his sudden height but too disturbed to comment.

"No, Aman," I choke.

"But how can we be together anywhere if I don't know anything about you?"

"My past shouldn't matter."

"Exactly," he says. "You can tell me anything." He brushes my cheek, the action sparking electricity beneath the skin and turning me into all nerves.

I truly have fallen for him. "Kiss me," I declare, needing to feel steady, predictable Aman against me. He leans down, bracing my face as his lips touch mine. His mouth is warm and soft. I breathe him in, enjoying the sensation. Our lips move as one.

He pulls back, and when I look up his left eye has a startling glint, a certain sparkle. I feel my stomach churn. Around me, everything seems to darken.

The trees begin to close in, leaving us sandwiched between them. The once peaceful dripping of the stream is now a strong roaring as the forest animals howl.

Aman's eyes darken, squinting into judgment. His new large nose crinkles, and his once lovely mouth turns into a grimace. He appears to expand before my eyes, his body bulging with muscles and pulsating with strength. It's him, his qualities on sweet Aman. But how can this be? I thought I was finally free of him. Arms wrap around me like a tight cage, drawing me to the true beast.

He roughly attacks my mouth as his large hands dance in a direction of their own. Hard. Fierce. Angry.

I push against his muscled chest to get free, but he pulls me tighter. I bite his lip; however, he seems to take the gesture as encouragement. I close my eyes and shut down, allowing the only one I trusted to take the little that is left of me.

The onslaught continues before he finally takes a breath, whispering threateningly into my ear, "You can never escape, Cassandra."

I scream, using all of my strength to push him away. Startled, he falls back. I dart and leap into the stream, daring just one glimpse back. I shriek, surprised to find my Aman once more: gentle, kind, and soft. His short hair, button nose, and light blue eyes. Even his just slightly too big hands.

"Cass?" Aman questions, clearly confused. "Did I do something wrong?"

"I am not ready," I cry, turning into the stream and swimming away from everything. From everyone. I thought I could be free of it. I thought I was better.

But maybe he will never let me escape, just as he claimed two years ago.

The man I loved. The man I trusted. Did his breach of trust bring this on?

All of the questions? Or was it the kiss? The lines of reality are severely blurred, my imagination playing tricks on me. Maybe the elders are wrong, and the evil things aren't in the forest. Perhaps it is the fears we already encompass coming to haunt us once more.

Either way, I must continue to run from it all; for as long as it takes.

About the Author

Emilee Ceuninck is a sophomore at the University of Arizona majoring in psychology with minors in business administration and pre-law. Emilee is passionate about young adult literature, scouring out every new release. When she's not busy writing her own YA fantasy trilogy or thriller, she enjoys hiking, movies and sunny weather. In the future, she hopes to pursue a career in law and become a published author.

Adult Published Finalist

The Waters of Michigan
Malachi King

Carlson and Shelley picked their way along the deserted freeway that was choked with smashed cars and jagged piles of rubble. They were talking about something other than the comet, anything but that, and it came back to the same argument as always. What was the worst thing to happen to the human race? Their voices bounced off the pavement in front of them and echoed in the silence of an exterminated city.

"Van Gogh's gun," Shelley said, a swarthy brunette in her twenties.

"Imagine it. Brought down all that creative talent."

"Fine then. How about Plato's hemlock? Beat that," Carlson replied. He was older than her but walked with downcast eyes and his movements were slow. The work of surviving had begun to overwhelm him.

Shelley acknowledged Carlson had a point. "Fine," she said. "I'll bet you Thirty-Second to Wall Street the next faker will say the gun was worse than your hemlock. What do you got?"

Carlson thought. "Maine. I bet Maine." He drained the last of his warm beer and chucked the can into a tumble of concrete.

"Screw Maine," Shelley said. "Michigan. Think of all that fresh water. You could live there. None of this." She swept her hand over the vehicle-clogged expressway, decayed and overgrown. The former skyscrapers were mostly toppled over amid a few empty steel shells standing in mock defiance. It was a mad man's playground, as if God had taken careful aim and blasted the earth with a cosmic sawed-off shot gun.

"Yeah," Carlson said. "Michigan. If only we could get there. How many times have we heard that?"

"Pipe dream. That's what it is. Probably doesn't exist anymore."

The sound of movement came to them. Someone was walking alone with a stick. You would always hear before you saw them when someone carried a stick. Travelers always banged on the empty cars before inspecting their insides. Rats had taken over all motor vehicles since the disaster. A bite from one of those suckers could lay you out with disease.

"Okay, get this," Carlson said, pushing thick glasses back up his nose.

"Rob Lowe's dirty sex tape!"

"How has that stopped progress?"

"Think of all the great movies he didn't make!"

"The comet was coming. There wasn't any more time."

A man appeared wearing a hood and using half a curtain rod as a cane. He spotted them and halted.

"Come here, faker," Shelley said. "We have a little wager going."

"So good to finally find someone," the man said, wheezing. "We could work together.

Everyone needs someone."

"No one falls for that anymore," Carlson said. "There's two of us, you don't stand a chance.

Besides, what you gonna to steal from us? Cigarette butts and tin cans?"

He laughed long and it echoed off the slanted concrete slabs.

"So, listen," Shelley said. "What do you think was a greater detriment to humanity: Plato's hemlock or Van Gogh's gun? I mean, c'mon, all Van Gogh did was paint a few pictures. Plato changed how we thought about ourselves. Am I right?"

The man eyed their belongings. The pockets of their backpacks bulged out temptingly. "We could walk together," he said. "For protection. And find some water."

Shelley shouted at him. "Tell us! What was more harmful? The hemlock or the painter's gun?" She fingered the bare metal of the handgun in her pocket and resisted the urge to blast the faker to kingdom come. Lately, she had found it increasingly difficult to resist the killing impulse.

"Strength in numbers," the man recited, "if we work together." He inched himself forward looking at the ground.

"Forget it, faker!" Shelley rushed forward and kicked the man in the stomach. A solid foot- punch right in the gut. He rolled to the ground and grunted like a sick dog. She reached down and pulled the hood away from his face. "Now we know you. Don't ever come near us again." Shelley pulled a few cigarettes from the man's pockets and walked away. Carlson followed.

They stepped around the corner, passed an old grocery store and then a bar. Carlson thought they would need new shoes again soon. The glass littering the sidewalks had torn their soles to shreds. At least the looters were mostly gone now.

"Are we going to Michigan now?" Carlson asked.

"Stop whining." Shelley's boots crunched the sidewalk ahead of him.

"And stop looking at my ass."

"I wasn't, Shelley. I swear I wasn't."

"Why the hell not?"

"I... I don't know. Maybe –"

"Shut it," Shelley said and waved it aside. "How about the Black Death? Imagine if all those people hadn't died. What kind of a world would we have now?"

Carlson thought they wouldn't be searching ruined buildings for food, that's what kind of world. You could usually find something – canned food, boxes of cereal, or anything in a sealed package – if you looked hard enough, but no one could travel far without running out of food.

"Smallpox," Carlson said. "It killed a lot. It was the worst – more than hemlock, Van Gogh's gun, and the Black Death combined."

Shelley didn't want to argue and turned down Westnedge Street. There wasn't much fear of the gangs anymore. You could always hear them. That's the thing in the post-comet world, the silence. You could hear everything.

"You're full of it, Carlson." Shelley was staring ahead. An old laundromat had a small nuclear sign partly hidden by greenery that seemed to sprout up everywhere, right out of the concrete. There must be an old bomb shelter in the basement. "C'mon. This way." Carlson followed her like a lost puppy.

Shelley had saved Carlson from a faker two weeks ago. He was slow sometimes, other times argumentative. He had PTSD, or Comet Shock, whatever you want to call it. Shelley had seen it among many survivors the first year. Now, in the second year, it was rare. People with Comet Shock just couldn't make it on their own. It took guts, instinct. You had to be aggressive.

Carlson just wanted to pet the dead rats he picked up. He said their fur was soft. And he wanted to talk.

"Native Americans didn't have a chance," Carlson said. "Sure, their weapons were inferior, but they dropped dead by the millions from smallpox. Bad for Monte, good for Cortez. Yeah, I vote for smallpox."

"Your wager?"

"The Mississippi."

"We'll ask the next faker."

Carlson stumbled and coughed. "Shelley?"

"Yeah?"

"Tell me about Michigan again. What will it be like?" Carlson stuck his hand inside his jacket pocket.

Shelley sighed. "There'll be water there. Lots of water. Sure, most of it will be dirty, but there are ten thousand lakes in Michigan, Carlson. I'm sure we could find one to drink from."

"And the farms? Are there farms there?"

"There are plenty of farms in Michigan. We could find some place away from the cities and live like royalty."

"Like royalty." Carlson smiled.

"Take that rat out of your pocket, Carlson. You're a pig, you know that? You're going to get us both sick."

"I don't have no rat, Shelley."

"You're a fuggin' liar. If you don't chuck it, I'm going to leave you behind."

The rat fell to the sidewalk.

"I don't see the harm..."

"You never do."

Carlson sniffed. "I'm hungry, Shelley. Really hungry."

Shelley rubbed her temples. "I know, Carlson. I'm sorry. Let's look in here."

They had reached the laundromat, brown and weathered with all the windows missing.

Shelley brushed some branches away, inspected the nuclear sign, and went inside.

There was always a chance someone had tried to hole up in a bomb shelter during The Panic. Everyone had simply gone crazy. The scientists had said the comet would hit the Southern Hemisphere, but it didn't. It broke into a thousand pieces all the size of Vermont and just laid waste.

They had five weeks' notice. How many lives can you save in five weeks?

On top of that, the atmospheric dust had circled the globe after the tsunamis ran their course. Most people survived only a month, three months if they were lucky. Some went into their basements if they had them.

Shelley's family even generated their own electricity while the gasoline lasted.

Inside the laundromat there were no clothes. Shelley didn't expect any.

They'd been cleared out long ago. But the bomb shelter might have escaped notice; the sign outside was hard to see.

She pushed her way to the back and found the manager's door ajar. There had been a fire; everything was black. A skeleton hunched in the corner. Died sometime after the fire, Shelley noted from the white of the bones.

Kneeling down, she tore away a few bits of charred carpet. Beneath, there was a hatch door, but it wouldn't budge. She called over Carlson, who pulled it open with ease. He smiled and went back to sit on a washing machine.

"Don't pick up any more rats, you hear?" Shelley called after him. "I'm going down to see if there's any food."

"Alright."

She stepped down the ladder rungs and let her eyes adjust to the poor light. There were a few tiny shelves and boxes. She rummaged around and only scored six cans of corn and two boxes of powdered milk. No water.

Someone had lived down here for a while. Someone who didn't like corn.

Carlson screamed from above.

Shelley dropped the cans and raced up the ladder. A faker in dirty rags held Carlson close to his body. He was grinning.

Shelley slowly raised and leveled her Glock 49 at him.

"Let him the fuck go." She stared into his dull eyes, set back in his dirty, grinning face. The man released Carlson, who slumped to the floor. The knife made a sickening slurp as Carlson's body pulled away from it. Blood ran from the blade down over the faker's hand.

"Easy now, little la–"

The shots rang out ONE – TWO – THREE in rapid succession. The faker's chest nearly came apart at the neck and shoulder and he collapsed on the tiles, surrounded by blood and gore.

Carlson groaned.

Shelley ran and turned him over. Blood spurted out of his chest. She tore off a piece of shirt and crammed it into the wound. She applied pressure and checked vitals. Breathing was low, heartbeat weak. She didn't bother searching the heavens for divine rescue; no one did anymore. It seemed enough hell had fallen from above already. But she did weep, long and from deep down.

By the time the fog cleared the next morning it was unusually late. That meant another season of dust was coming. Everyone had called it "pollution" at first, but you could see and feel the physical particles in the air. Dirt coated everything. The comet had thrown massive amounts of pulverized earth and stone into the atmosphere and the seasons had changed. Last year the fog lasted until eleven each morning on the East Coast until a dust hurricane really tore things up. People used to think Black Monday had been bad in Oklahoma. Now it was high noon and the fog had barely lifted.

Shelley fed Carlson some corn and a little water she found by digging next to a rogue willow tree by the next door apartment building. She had dug a hole until the soil was damp and put a towel in and then pushed the dirt back over it. In a day the towel was wet enough to wring a few cups of water from it. It was brown, but drinkable.

Shelley knew they couldn't stay here long. She wasn't afraid of more fakers; it was the dust storm she knew was coming. It was time to head west, out of the city. Food might be found along the way. A person couldn't live through a dust hurricane without filtration.

She looked at Carlson. He had sat up with difficulty and was chewing his food slowly, eyes bright again, but his body remained rigid. She replaced the stuffing in his knife wound with some fresh pieces of cloth. The wound was raw and ugly. The lips of the cut had recoiled from each other and his entire abdomen was bruised and swollen. A trickle of pus ran down his side and disappeared underneath him. And he had developed a fever.

Shelley sat down behind Carlson and rubbed his shoulders. Carlson watched the fog dissipate over the ruins of Westnedge Street. The storefronts were unrecognizable and he could see two skeletons in an old BMW across the street.

"Tell me about Michigan again, Shelley."

"I can't. You tell it."

"C'mon, you tell it so good."

Shelley sighed. "You know, Carlson, other people, they ain't got no family. People like that are the loneliest people on earth."

Carlson nodded and watched the fog.

"But not us," Shelley said. "We have a future. And we have each other to talk to. Other people can rot and no one gives a damn. But not us."

"Shelley, did I do a bad thing?"

"No, you didn't do a bad thing."

"You told me not to trust the fakers."

"You didn't do a bad thing."

"He said he wanted to help me."

"I know." Shelley pulled her backpack close and found another can inside it. She opened the can and gave it to Carlson. He shoved the food in his mouth with dirty fingers. The fog blew completely away with the increasing wind.

"What're we going to do in Michigan, Shelley?" "We're going to find some water –"

"And a farm!"

"Yes, and a farm."

Shelley pulled the Glock from her backpack. She set it in her lap and let herself cry. "Can we grow corn in Michigan?" Carlson asked.

"We will grow lots of corn. There's ten thousand lakes in Michigan. Some of them are bound to be clean."

"We can live there forever, can't we?"

"Yes, forever."

The wind was stronger now. A sound like rain pelted the roof and she knew it was the beginning of the dust storm. "Shelley?"

"Yes?" She raised the gun, but couldn't steady it. She let it rest in her lap again. "What animals can we have?"

"Cows for milk... Rabbits for meat..."

Carlson started to turn his head, but winced from the pain.

"Just look across the road," Shelley said. "Can you imagine it? Our farm?"

"Just us and no one else."

"We can live –"

"Off the fatta the land!" Carlson giggled.

"Yes." Shelley raised the gun again and put both hands on it. She leveled the muzzle close behind Carlson's head.

"When are we going, Shelley?" "Soon. Very soon."

"Me and you?"

"You and me."

"Let's go now, Shelley. Right now."

The blast rang out with terrible force and swept up and down the deserted street in echoing waves. The wind finally carried it away with the rolling thunder of the storm. Carlson's head slumped forward on his chest and his body relaxed.

Shelley rocked herself back and forth on her heels, head down, arms wrapped around her knees. It felt like her mother was holding her again, eons ago, and both were wrapped in an Afghan blanket by the fireplace.

Daddy was in his chair smoking a pipe and laughing.

After a time, Shelley gathered her supplies and pocketed the gun. She laid Carlson's jacket over his face and straightened his body out in funeral style. Then she wrapped one of her shirts around her head, covering her mouth and nose. Outside, the hellish whirlwind stung her exposed skin.

Without pausing, she turned down Westnedge and headed west. Maybe even as far as the waters of Michigan.

END

About the Author

Malachi King is a U.S. Air Force veteran and holds a Language Arts degree from Grand Valley State University. He writes about emotion, survival, and courage. Malachi has minor works published in various markets including the national magazine "Mensa Bulletin" and has short stories published as ebooks by Untreed Reads Publishers available through Amazon and Barnes and Noble.

Adult Published Finalist

The Leader of the Pack
Avery Saylor

The stairs were the first sign of a problem. For years he would follow the family from the basement to the first floor to the top story, keeping pace with any one of them, despite his short stature. Truth be told he'd be glad to go up any number of stairs to stay with the pack. If they were doing laundry, he would watch; a dirty pile of clothes made the best resting place anyway.

If they were cooking, he would be perfectly content to stand by their feet waiting for the inevitable morsel of food to be dropped to the floor where he could scarf it down before they had a chance to grab it away. Nighttime was the best though, they loved to watch the screen, a sprawl of velvety blankets laid out before him with the choice of any lap to fall asleep on, and then up the stairs to bed. But not anymore.

He couldn't remember when it had started exactly, it was gradual. Every day the strain of going up and down became a little harder. His knees hurt, he couldn't catch his breath, he felt tired. Sometimes mom or dad would carry him if they needed him to come along. After all, he knew they wouldn't be able to fall asleep without him there to protect them. But the quick trips to the basement, followed by going on long walks, and then even standing in the kitchen for dinner became too much. He just wanted to sleep.

The girls still threw his toy for him, the stuffed rabbit that had always been his favorite. It wasn't what it used to be, but mom had patched it up enough times to keep the fluff from falling out despite the missing ear and torn paw. He remembered when he had gotten the rabbit, it had been the same day he had met the oldest girl. After an extended absence of mom and dad in which he thought they might never come home, they had returned with a new being. In the years following the oldest girl would grow far taller than him and run much faster, but at their earliest introduction, he wasn't sure of what to make of the small relatively motionless thing in front ofhim.

All he knew was that mom and dad had placed a stuffed rabbit near her for him, which he took with appreciation, and that he felt the urge to care for the new addition. Another girl had followed a few years later, and he loved her just as much. He thought fondly on the times they had played together, the treats they had shared, the comfortable naps they had taken.

They threw his bunny down the hall and urged him to go after it. Heavily he pulled himself up and trudged after it, dropping the toy at their feet before returning to his bed. They gave him a loving pat before walking away, leaving him to rest.

It was that night that he watched in confusion as the family went up the stairs to bed like always, but instead of dad picking him up, he had been left behind. He waited anxiously by the base of the stairs, a soft whimper escaping from his muzzle for hours after it went dark to not wake them.

Eventually, he curled up on the hardwood landing, unable to get to the top himself. There were many pets and apologies in the morning, but it didn't take away the hurt he felt. He realized they were able to fall asleep without him. Something until then he had thought to be impossible.

The accidents came soon after. He was a good boy, he knew that. He had been told so many times since he was small, but now he was bad. It wasn't on purpose. It couldn't be controlled. The shame he felt as he snuck away after an accidental piddle was unbearable. He didn't mean to be bad. He was sorry.

The girls still gave him cuddles, but there weren't as many as before.

And they had completely given up trying to play fetch anymore. What was happening to him?

The new being came within a month of the accidents starting. It looked different than the girls had. It was smaller, yet it could move much faster. It sped and slid around corners with more agility than even they could. It had seemingly unlimited energy and would chase the girls up and down the stairs several times in an hour, a happy panting grin on its face the whole time. All he could do was watch from his bed; his joints too achy to join in. The family would take them on walks together sometimes, but he just couldn't keep up, and dad would have to carry him home as the rest of the family went on without him.

It was cute. Quite honestly, cuter than the girls had been when mom and dad first brought them home, it looked like him. It acted like he used to act. He realized he was being replaced.

It was a difficult realization. The girls wanted to see the new "puppy" after school instead of him, dad went outside to play fetch after work without him, and even mom, who had been his first companion so long ago could be found cuddling on the couch with the new thing. But as the tiredness took up more of his day, and the pain got worse he knew it would do him no good to deny the truth.

Mom and Dad were at work, the girls were at school, and the new puppy was upstairs in the crate. Mustering his strength, he pulled himself from the bed and went to the base of the stairs. Slowly he made his way up, one at a time, each step causing his short legs to cry in pain and his breath to become shallower. At the top, he staggered into the girls' room and saw the puppy greet him excitedly in its cage. This new animal would do a good job, he felt it. He trudged over to the cage, his lungs beginning to give out, and dropped what he had carried all the way up out of his mouth: the rabbit.

Nudging it over to the new owner, he gave a diminished howl of approval before descending back down the stairs to his bed to take one last good nap.

They would be okay without him. He had done his job well. He was a good boy.

About the Author

Avery Saylor lives in St. Joseph, Michigan. When she isn't doing community theater, crocheting, knitting or reading, she is pursuing her dream of being an author. The inspiration for this short story is credited to her husband, who suggested a look at a relationship between an old dog and a new one. As someone who loves animals and has lost beloved childhoods pets, she was inspired by the concept. She hopes you enjoy the story, and that you'll be reading more from her in the future!

Teen Judges' Choice Winner

A Paradise Past
Cassie Peckens

It's drafty in the theater. The air smells of wood, paint, sweat, and melted makeup. The buzzing spotlights nearly blind me, and the house is dark and empty, eerie with silence. It is just me, standing center stage, wishing for a paradise past.

I reach out, and the house fills with people. The audience gapes as I take a huge breath and belt the final high note of the song, my emerald ball gown glittering with jewels and my skin glimmering with sweat. The orchestra cuts out. All eyes are on me. I am alive.

Heart pounding, eyes glistening with tears, I cut off the note. I close my eyes and wait for the theater, once again, to erupt in deafening applause...

A knock at the door shatters my memory. The lights dim; the house is silent. It's drafty in the theater. It truly is just me, standing alone at center stage. It truly is just me, with an elderly body that can no longer dance and a lost voice that will never sing again. It truly is just me, wishing for a paradise past.

The door opens, and the lead of the high school show pokes in her blonde head. "Hello, Ms. Director? Um, I know rehearsals haven't started yet, but I have some questions about my lines..."

Another memory flashes across my mind. On opening night, I tremble offstage. It's my cue to enter, but I can't move. My legs wobble like rubber and my heart pounds like a timpani. On stage, the other main characters glance at me and start to improvise, giving me time.

But I can't move. My co-stars are phenomenal actors; they know internally how to make the audience laugh, their chemistry is legendary, and they never miss a beat. But I'm just me—awkward, clumsy, inadequate.

I've never made it through a rehearsal without messing up. I shouldn't be playing the lead. I shouldn't even be here.

I turn to leave, but a warm hand clasps my shoulder. "Hey," my director says, beaming at me. "Look at how far you've come. You can do this."

Those simple words are all I need. My panic melts into a smile, and I walk on stage.

Back in the present, a revived passion unfurls within my heart like a blazing flower. I'm not the lead anymore, no, and this young, timid star can't shine on her own. She needs a director.

"Of course, my dear," I say. "What can I help you with?"

About the Author

Cassie Peckens is a homeschooled high school senior who loves to sing, act, play instruments, and spend time with her friends and family. She is the Senior President of her homeschool co-op. She also serves in leadership positions in her advanced choir classes and in the National Honor Society of her online school. English/writing has always been her favorite school subject; she has taken many writing classes throughout high school simply for the fun of it. She is excited to experience and explore the wonderful opportunities college has to offer.

Teen Judges' Choice Runner-Up

Snow & Silence
Katherine Blackwell

We walk straight past the chain link fence, our shoes crunching in the cover of snow. It shouldn't, but it makes my stomach drop. It feels like we shouldn't be here- like we'd certainly get in trouble for being here, especially so late at night. And yet, there's nothing to stop us. There's no camera, no lock, not even a gate for a lock to go on. All that stands between us and our old elementary school is a gap in the fence.

The place where I spent the first half of my childhood stretches out before me, dusted in white. It's all here: the same monkey bars where I had the wind knocked out of me for the first time; the field where the sporty kids would play soccer every day; the rope ladder everyone dared each other to jump off of because it seemed so tall when we were that little. A combination of moonlight and reflective snow casts it all in a pale haze, dulling the already faded paint.

Corey elbows me lightly, and I turn to look at him. He's smiling, a cast of humor shining in his eyes. "Do you want to race to the swings?" he asks, his words filling the air between us with vapor.

A grin tugs at my own face. Already I can feel my legs tensing, longing to make a break for it and dash across the playground like I used to. "It's all snowy, it'll be slippery," I reply in weak protest. "There might be ice."

"So?" he asks.

We both stare at each other for a moment, smiling. Then, he pushes my shoulder and shoots off towards the swingset. Laughing, I scramble after him. "False start, you jerk!"

Something childish wells up in me, a kind of excitement, the joy of the vague recklessness of racing with a friend. The wind I create presses my shirt flat against my body and adds a fresh sting of cold to my nose and cheeks. For those ten seconds where Corey and I are running across the old playground, I feel something like freedom. We don't exist in a place where time flows, or where I have to wake up tomorrow and think about scholarships and college applications. For ten seconds, all I have to do is run and laugh, with the moon as my witness.

Corey skids to a halt first, tossing out an arm to stop himself against a red-painted pole; tarnished black metal shows through chips in the paint. I stumble past him to catch myself on the chains of a swing. It rattles violently, startled awake by my rough landing. The cold metal bites at my hands, and the seat whips back at me, knocking into my knees. It hurts, and I know I'll have a bruise there tomorrow, but I push the sensation aside and turn to face Corey.

We're both still grinning, both panting a little, creating miniature clouds in the cool night air. A certain vitality shines out from him in the red of his cheeks and the energized gleam in his eyes. I wonder if I look like him right now. I sort of hope I do. "I so beat you," he says.

"Yeah, you did," I laugh back because I don't know what else to say.

Instead of speaking more, I turn, sit on the swing, and start kicking.

Corey walks behind me and sits down on the next swing over, following my lead. For a while, we're silent. We swing back and forth, falling in and out of sync, listening to the familiar creak of the old chains. After a minute or two, I close my eyes, and I can almost believe that I'm eight again, playing during recess like any normal day. For a few moments, I pretend that I'm back in second grade, that the sun is high in the sky and there isn't a care in the world besides who's playing with who and which teachers were mean this week. College is imaginary, and the next ten years are eternal.

Then I open my eyes, and my made-up world falls away. I'm just a 17-year-old with a mind full of questions and fears playing in an empty playground in the middle of the night. It takes the wind out of my sails, and I stop kicking so hard, letting myself slow.

Corey drags his feet until he fully stops. "What are you thinking about?" he asks.

I scrape my boots against the ground to stop and watch as the woodchips scatter. It suddenly makes me wonder if the school has replaced them or topped them off since we've gone here. In the six years I've been away, could they have covered up or thrown out the very same woodchips I used to walk on nearly every day? Or are these the same, still bearing the memory of my first pair of laced shoes?

I let the silence linger for a while longer, staring at the woodchips and thinking. Corey waits, his body angled towards me in the swing. When I do finally speak, it's not quite about what's bothering me, but it's the closest thing to it that I can make come out of my mouth. "It's weird to think that there was a year where we both went here and we didn't know each other."

He's quiet for a few beats, then says, "I mean, it was only my first year here and we were a grade apart. It makes sense."

I shove the tip of my shoe into the woodchips and agitate a line back and forth. "No, I know that," I force out, feeling awkward. Why is it so hard to speak? "Obviously, it makes sense that we didn't talk. It's just weird. We went to the same school every day for nine whole months and I doubt we ever even looked at each other. That is weird." I dig my toe in deeper, preparing myself for what I want to say next. "And it's kind of frustrating, you know? Like, imagine if we'd been able to become friends back then. We'd be so much closer right now. That's a lot of memories that we'll never get to have. It's just...it's just a little bit sad." Nerves flip around in my stomach as I wait for a response. I keep my eyes locked on the woodchips so I don't have to see Corey's reaction.

"I think," he starts slowly, as though thinking through his words, "that it's okay that we lost out on that time." I peek up again as he continues, relieved to find him looking more towards the school than towards me. "We were just kids, we weren't really us yet. I think the fact that we get to be friends now, when we're the best people we've ever been, and that we get to tell each other all of the stories from that time, makes up for the fact that we didn't get to spend that time together. Plus, as I said, if it was so unlikely to happen, it's not worth being sad about. We're friends now and that's what matters."

Finished, he looks back at me for my reaction. A sprinkle of snow's begun to fall, and the tiny flakes stick to his honey-blond hair as he gazes back at me steadily. "I guess you're right," I say. A small smile tugs at my lips. We're friends.

"Of course I'm right," he says, extending a leg to tap my shin with his shoe.

I cut him a glare, but a smile quickly overtakes it, and then we're both grinning at each other again.

"Glad we're friends," I say.

"Me too."

The snow picks up, and I look to the sky as it falls in fluffy flakes. Corey looks too. They cling to my hair and clothe s and get stuck to my eyelashes.

It's absolutely beautiful, all of that white floating down so gently from so dark a sky. Time ceases again, and this time all that matters is silently staring up at the snow with my friend, soaking in the scene. I try to take a picture of it in my mind and hope I'll remember it when I'm older.

I think about what Corey said about how us being friends now matters, and wonder if maybe this is part of what he meant. We get to be here sharing this moment– this snow and this silence– together. How could anything else possibly matter?

About the Author

Katherine J. Blackwell is a teen writer who primarily enjoys writing stories about the beauty of everyday life and human experiences. She's been an avid reader and writer since first grade when a story in the fantasy genre sparked her love for books. Though she still loves reading fantasy, most of her works now center on descriptive scenes that strive to capture beautiful moments inspired by nature and her own life. She hopes to one day be a librarian and self-publish books on the side.

Teen Readers' Choice Winner
The World Moves On Around Us
Anjali Sardar

She's flying up the hill, practically defying gravity, her thick braid thumping irregularly against her back in a way I'm certain is going to leave a bruise. Either that, or the pink plastic lunchbox she's carrying, which is beating a tattoo into her leg with every step. She doesn't seem to notice either of them, though, which is classic Sophie. A gust of wind could knock her over—this is speaking from experience—but she keeps plowing forward like a very small, very blonde bull.

"Come on, Tommy!" she urges, glancing back at me, her blue eyes sparkling with a fever of excitement. "Hurry!"

I groan, quickening my pace, the red wagon I'm dragging behind me opposing my lackluster effort. But there's a magnetic quality about Sophie when she's excited, a quality that makes me drop whatever I'm doing and go along with her. Which is how I ended up dragging my red wagon full of our things up the hill after her. She's at the top of the hill now, bouncing up and down on the balls of her feet. I have to laugh.

"Soph, do you ever stop moving?"

"Nope!" she laughs, still bouncing. She reminds me of a shaken soda can sometimes, her energy bubbling over uncontrollably. The wild blonde curls she keeps confined to a low braid only add to the image in my head. Right now, some strands have escaped, forming a frizzy sort of halo around her face. Just as I notice it, she pushes the strands down, jogging over to help me with the wagon. We take the last stretch of the hill together, hauling the wagon over the final ridge and letting it go, then dropping down to sit in the grass. Sophie keeps one eye on it.

"Not the best place we could have left it," she says, grinning at me. "We don't want it ending up like me."

We both snicker at the memory of six-year-old Sophie getting knocked over by a gust of wind, tumbling halfway down the hill before I managed to grab hold of her. Thinking about it never fails to make us laugh. I shoot her a mischievous grin.

"I think the wagon weighs more than you, Soph."

She shrieks in mock outrage, then jumps on me, tackling me to the ground. We end up wrestling in the grass until we lay side by side in the grass, breathless with laughter and exertion, staring up at the sky. The sun seems impossibly bright. For a while, we're both content to just be there, beside each other in that moment, no words needed, just hearing the sound of each other breathing as the world moves on around us. Finally, Sophie breaks the silence.

"Are you ready?"

We both push ourselves to our feet, and Sophie grabs the wagon, pulling it over to the lone tree on top of the hill.

"I still don't see why we had to use those ones," I say, following her with the lunchbox.

Sophie insisted on bringing our dads' shovels in the wagon. I'll admit they're technically more efficient for what we have in mind, but the one hitch in the plan is that they're about a head taller than Sophie.

"And I still don't see why not," she replies, flashing that contagious smile at me over her shoulder. "Live a little, Tommy."

This is where Sophie and I are different. She likes to take on the impossible, which makes me crazy. I like to play it safe, which drives her nuts. After we've dug the hole (which takes a lot longer than it should have thanks to certain harebrained ideas), I pass her the lunchbox, and she puts it in the hole, then stands back and looks at me.

"You first or me?"

"You," I say. This whole thing was her idea. She takes it out of the wagon and holds it up for me to see.

"Remember this?"

I grin. "I'm not likely to forget it."

It's a picture of Sophie and me on our first day of kindergarten. Her mom had made her leave her hair down, but the moment we were alone, she had begged me to braid it for her. I had done my best, and the result was a tight, but very crooked braid. Everyone had given her funny looks for the rest of the day, but she had refused to take it out. At the end of the day, my mom had taken a picture of the two of us, Sophie with her crooked braid, and me, proud of my handiwork.

"I'm better at braiding now," I add.

Sophie laughs. "Yeah, you definitely are. I loved that one, though." She kneels, putting the picture in the box, then stands back, brushing dirt off her hands.

"Your turn, Tommy."

I chose a picture, too, this one more recent. Sophie's older brother, Noah, took it last fall, after our grade's performance of The Wizard of Oz. Sophie was the Wicked Witch of the West, and I was the Cowardly Lion. Noah got a picture of us after the first performance, Sophie still green and witchy, me still in my lion outfit, both of us beaming for the camera. She grins at the sight of the picture, and I put it in the box, shutting the lid. Sophie kicks dirt over it, then turns to me.

"So now we wait."

"Twenty years, right?" I ask. I'm a little skeptical about that, but it's what she told me. "Twenty years," she confirms, her eyes shining. "We'll come back here when we're twenty-eight and open the box."

She sticks out her hand and we shake on it.

Ten Years Later "Are you sure you don't want to change your mind?"

I sigh. We've been over this at least ten times in as many hours. "No, Soph. I'm not changing my mind."

Her right knee bounces up and down, hitting the steering wheel of her car in a regular rhythm. She still can't sit still for more than a minute. "There's still an option, though, right?"

"Soph."

Now it's her turn to sigh, blue eyes turning heavenward, the way they always do when she's emotional. "Sorry, Tommy. I'm just worried."

She rakes a hand through her curls, which are in their normal braid, but with the usual stray strands flying out around her face. Some things never change, I think idly, watching her for a moment. She still reminds me of a shaken soda can. The difference is that today, it's all anxious energy. The bouncing knee, incessant fidgeting with her hair—they're all her nervous habits. I used to see them before history tests and performances, and most recently, when she got her college acceptance letters. Today, though, she's nervous for me. After we graduated high school, I deferred college in favor of enlisting in the Air Force. Sophie's been a nervous wreck since the day I told her.

"I know," I tell her. "But I'm going to be fine. It's just basic training."

"Yeah, but what happens after basic training?" she counters. "I'm proud of you, Tommy, but I don't—" She cuts herself off abruptly. "Never mind. Forget I said anything. I'm sorry."

I nod, but I'm already finishing her sentence in my head. I'm proud of you, Tommy, but I don't want you to die.

"Nothing's going to happen to me, Soph."

She opens her mouth, "you don't know that" about to fly out, then shuts it again. I tug on the end of her braid, the way I used to when we were kids.

"I need to come back in ten years so we can dig up that time capsule, remember?"

She laughs in spite of herself, and I see a little bit of the old sparkle coming back into her eyes.

"Yeah, we still need to do that."

The sparkle is short-lived, though. She glances at the time lit up in bright white letters on her dashboard, and I can see the light in her eyes dim slightly.

"You should go if you want to make it to your flight in time."

I glance at the time and slump back against my seat, disappointed. She's right. I need to be at the gate two hours before the flight, and right now, I only have half an hour to make it there.

"I probably should," I say regretfully. If it were up to me, I would never leave the car, my plane would never take off, and we would just be here, like we had been on the day we had buried the time capsule. Just hearing the sound of each other breathing as the world moves on around us. But we're not children anymore. I get out of the car and after a moment's hesitation, Sophie follows. We stand in front of the car, neither of us ready to initiate what we know has to come next. Finally, Sophie does.

"Stay safe, okay?" she says, not looking at me, but somewhere on the pavement to my left. "Okay."

She smiles at me, a little sadly, even though she's trying to hide it. "I'm going to miss you, Tommy."

"I'm going to miss you, too, Soph."

She stands on tiptoe to kiss my cheek, our normal form of a goodbye that doesn't require actually saying the word. At the same time, I turn my head, intending to do the same to her, and our lips meet in the middle. It's brief, barely a second, but turns into long enough to send us both stumbling backward, cheeks flaming and stammered apologies tumbling over each other.

"God, Soph, I'm so sorry!"

"I'm sorry, Tommy, I don't know what that was!"

We fall silent, still staring at each other. It's suddenly a little harder to breathe.

"I'm . . ." Sophie stammers, clearly still flustered. "I'm going to . . . you know . . . never mind. Have a safe flight, Tommy."

She jumps into her car and is halfway across the parking lot before I can even open my mouth. "Soph . . ." I start, then stop. I run my fingers through my hair, pushing the stray strands out of my face before I pick up my bag, which Sophie had dropped on the ground in part of her mad rush to get away from me, and head into the airport to catch my flight.

Ten Years Later

She's standing at the top of the hill, hands jammed into the pockets of her jeans, leaning all her weight on her right leg. Her sleeves are rolled up to the elbows, and her frizzy blonde curls are confined to a low braid. She looks exactly the same, but somehow not the same at all. Something about her is harder. More . . . experienced, in a way, like she's seen a lot of life in a short time. Her gaze travels over me, taking in the regulation haircut and the camouflage uniform. All traces of the boy she once knew, gone.

"Tommy," she says. Her voice has no emotion, no inflection, but it's almost like she's asking me if I'm still there. If I'm still the same person she used to know.

"Soph."

The sound of her old nickname seems to strike a chord in her. She flinches, biting her lip. That worldly hardness gone, replaced by uncertainty. I rarely saw this side of Sophie, but it hurt every time. It hurts even more to see it because of me.

"You remembered," she finally says. Simple. Direct. Safe. Not going to lead to any awkward conversations of the incident at the airport ten years ago.

"Yeah," I reply.

Silence. Not the comfortable silence we used to have when we sat here as kids. An awkward, loaded silence, full of ten years worth of unasked questions and words left unsaid. In those ten years, I don't know how many letters I've started with "Soph", then erased and started with someone else's name. I never knew what to write. An apology? A confession? Pretend it never happened and go on with our lives? Her knee is jackhammering, just like that day where it smacked repeatedly against the steering wheel. A few curls have escaped her braid and are framing her face like a frizzy sort of halo, just like that day when we buried the box and promised to come back in twenty years. She clears her throat awkwardly, dispelling whatever the moment was.

"Should we . . ." She gestures at the shovels on the ground by her feet. For the next few minutes, there are no more words exchanged. We both dig, simultaneously acknowledging and ignoring each other as we wait for one of our shovels to hit pink plastic. Finally, hers does. She pulls the box from the earth, setting it down between us and flicking the catch open. Four sets of eyes stare up at us from inside. A Wicked Witch and a Cowardly Lion, both seven years old. Two kindergarteners fresh from their first day, one with a crooked braid, and the other exceedingly proud of the job he did. Sophie's lips quirk up into something that's almost a smile.

"Glad to see you got better at braiding."

"Hey, I was five!" I defend myself. "And it was my first time. I think I did okay!"

She makes a "so-so" gesture with her hand, but her smile is growing. It's like old times, before the "Weird Airport Incident", as I've been calling it in my head.

"You're thinking about the airport thing, right?"

I look up at her so quickly I nearly get whiplash. "What?"

She shakes her head, still grinning at me. "Tommy, we may not have spoken in ten years, but I knew you for eighteen. I can practically read your mind. I was thinking about it, too."

I start what is probably going to be a long-winded apology, but she cuts me off. "I know what you're going to say, but let's not go there. You're going to be nervous and stammer, then I'm going to be awkward and ramble, and we'll both end up not talking for another ten years because we'll never actually have gotten to talk about anything here, right?"

There's no point in arguing, because she is right. I have a tendency to be nervous and stammering when I apologize, and she has a tendency to awkwardly ramble when she apologizes. The route I almost started us on will get us nowhere, which is exactly where we've been for the last ten years.

"Yeah, you're right."

I see that hint of a smile again before she continues. "So can we skip the whole apology thing and go back to my place like we used to?"

"Okay," I reply, hiding a grin. "I can't go to your place, though."

Her brow furrows in confusion. "What? Why not?"

The grin finally breaks through. It's been too long since I pulled one over Sophie. "Noah." That's all I need to say. Noah is a stereotypical protective older brother when it comes to Sophie. Him and me being in the same place so soon after the Airport Incident (and yes, ten years is soon when it comes to Noah) is probably not the best idea. Sophie laughs, all too aware of what Noah is like.

"Okay, I'll give you that. Your place?"

"In the same house as my mother?"

She rolls her eyes, but she's laughing. "Okay, okay. Here is fine."

"I don't know," I tease, pretending to be picky. "I don't want you getting blown over by the wind."

She smacks my arm. "That was twenty-two years ago! I've grown since then!"

"You have," I concede, still grinning like an idiot. It's good to have the old Sophie back.

"How much, though . . ."

That earns me another smack on the arm. Sophie may only be five foot two to my six foot one, but she packs a punch. I pretend to be in way more pain than she actually caused, and she rolls her eyes at me. Hours later, we end up lying on our backs in the grass, tired from laughing even after all this time. Just hearing the sound of each other breathing as the world moves on around us.

About the Author

Anjali is a seventeen-year-old junior in high school. She is a Hufflepuff who enjoys writing and reading. Her favorite genres to both read and write are realistic fiction and fantasy. Her literary inspirations are Aaron Sorkin, and her uncle, Anurag Andra, who is also a writer.

Teen Spanish Language Winner

El Sacrificio de los Zodiacos
Yolihuani Dietachmayr

¿Te has preguntado alguna vez por qué están las constelaciones del zodiaco en el cielo?

Hace mucho, mucho tiempo, cuando el mundo era joven, las personas vivieron en un mundo sin color. Los dioses antiguos del zodiaco se despertaban todos los días y veían ante ellos los árboles, las plantas, la ropa y hasta el cabello, en blanco y negro. El mundo era triste, y todos sentían como que les faltaba algo. Cada noche miraban el cielo, la única cosa que tenía color en la tierra, observaban las estrellas, y deseaban poder hacer algo para que su tierra fuera más colorida. Un día, el zodiaco más valiente, Aries, decidió embarcarse en una misión para encontrar el color. Los otros zodiacos lo siguieron para ayudarlo.

Su plan era hablar con la diosa del espacio, Astrea, y preguntarle si ella les podría prestar un poco de su color para la tierra.

Pronto llegaron a la playa Aequoral, un lugar sagrado para ellos, justo donde estaba el océano. Los 12 zodiacos entraron al agua e hicieron un círculo, juntando sus poderes de los 4 elementos para llamar a la diosa Astrea.

Agua, viento, fuego y tierra eran uno en el circulo mágico. Así esperaron pacientemente, cayendo en un trance, hasta que Astrea los llamó.

Como no pudo bajarse del cielo, Astrea tuvo que visitarlos en sus sueños.

Cuando los zodiacos abrieron sus ojos, estaban flotando en el espacio rodeados de estrellas por todos lados donde miraban.

Una muchacha con ojos que brillantes y cabello largo que se veía como una galaxia, apareció frente a ellos.

- Bienvenidos queridos zodiacos. ¿Por qué están aquí? - dijo Astrea Cáncer fue el primero que habló.

 - A nuestra tierra la falta color y estábamos pensando que nos pudieras compartir un poco de tu magia del cielo para darle color a nuestro mundo.

La diosa lo contempló.

- Si puedo… pero a cambio quiero algo - contestó Astrea. Los zodiacos se pusieron a discutir entre ellos.

-Qué tenemos para dar? - preguntó Acuario.

Se miraron los unos a los otros.

- Le podríamos dar uno de nuestros tesoros, como el diamante blanco -dijo Virgo.

-Quiza le gustaría que contruyeramos una ofrenda para ella? - propuso Leo. Astrea los interrumpió diciendo.

- No hay necesidad de discutir, yo ya sé lo que quiero de ustedes.

Todos se callaron, esperando las palabras de la diosa.

- En el espacio, necesitamos a las estrellas para proteger a los mundos. Hay muy pocas aquí arriba. Si ustedes aceptan convertirse en constelaciones, le daré color a la tierra.

- Pero vamos a poder regresar a la tierra? No quiero abandonar a mis amigos los peces -pregunto Piscis.

- Eventualmente, sí, pero tu lealtad es para el cielo. Hablen entre ustedes para decidir - contestó Astrea.

Los zodiacos discutieron otra vez.

- Las futuras generaciones podrán vivir en un mundo de color - dijo Libra.

Después de unos minutos más, decidieron qué hacer.

- Bueno, nosotros aceptamos, pero solo si podemos visitar la tierra, cada año. - dijo Aries.

- Asi sera - dijo Astrea. Movió su mano y los mandó a casa.

Cuando los zodiacos abrieron sus ojos, vieron que el mundo estaba lleno de color. El océano era azul, el bosque estaban lleno de color, el pasto era verde, y cuando vieron su reflexión en el agua, se dieron cuenta que ellos también tenían color. ¡Que maravilla! - pensaron.

Leo se admiró en el agua, contenta con su cabello que se veía como el fuego.

- Soy tan hermosa - les dijo. Los otros se rieron.

Unos zodiacos fueron a disfrutar la comida, que ahora tenía color.

Los zodiacos de la tierra, Tauro, Virgo y Capricornio, estaban muy contentos con su jardín, que ahora estaba lleno de flores coloridas. Los del agua, Cáncer, Escorpio y Piscis, nadaban en el océano fresco que ahora era azul en lugar de blanco. Los del Fuego, Aries, Leo y Sagitario, empezaron a preparar comida con fuego de todos colores. Los zodiacos del Aire, Gemini, Libra y Acuario, no podían ver el viento, pero disfrutaron de todas las otras maravillas que ahora tenían color.

Después de su último día en la tierra, los zodiacos regresaron con Astrea y protegieron el espacio, convirtiendose en constelaciones de animales.

¿Alguna vez has visto un cangrejo, o un pez? Seguramente son Cancer y Piscis, que siguen aquí con nosotros. Los zodiacos están por todos lados, en los elementos, los animales, los colores. Por su sacrificio, nuestra vida está llena de color.

About the Author

Yolihuani Dietachmayr Gonzalez is a twelve-year-old girl born and raised in Michigan by a Mexican mother and an Austrian father. In her free time she enjoys writing, watching TV, and above all, reading. Her writing usually consists of fantasy stories and realistic fiction. "El Sacrificio de los Zodiacos" is her first short story written in Spanish.

Teen Published Finalist

Painted Feathers
Molly Bilbey

There was once a duck in the middle of a pond, at the edge of a park, in a small town. But he was no ordinary duck. He was a decoy. Just a poor little statue. No one admired him like they did the other ducks, no one named him, no one even gave him a second glance. He was all right for a while, but a long enough time of being ignored will wear down even the strongest of spirits. And after years of this dejection, he was pretty worn down.

"Why can't I be a real duck?" he would often wonder. "Why doesn't anyone care about the decoy?"

It just wasn't fair.

He would sit in the pond and watch the other ducks as they ate breadcrumbs and other tidbits given to them by the adoring people. He would watch the other ducks as they swam up to the people, sometimes even venturing on shore to waddle up to them. The people always gave them extra breadcrumbs for that. After years of watching from afar, the decoy decided he would be a decoy no longer. He was going to be a real duck.

The decoy floated to the edge of the pond with purpose. He floated back and forth, mimicking the other ducks. He floated closer and closer to the people, but none of them seemed to notice. So, he decided to get up on the shore. But when he finally reached solid ground, one of the people muttered something about the wind and put him back in the pond.

"Maybe being a duck just isn't my destiny." He considered. "Maybe I'm supposed to be something else entirely. I don't know what yet. Perhaps some exploring would do me good." And so the decoy went to explore places he had never been.

He wandered into the woods, marveling at the towering trees and babbling brooks. Eventually, he reached a clearing where some people were having a picnic. He noticed a sparrow in a tree nearby singing a lovely song, and he saw how the people admired it and enjoyed its tune.

"Perhaps I should be a sparrow," He contemplated. "I could sing to people and entertain them, then I would be appreciated."

So, he resolved to be a sparrow. He crept up to the people until he was close enough to be heard. He opened his plastic beak and let out a noise.

It was a terrible scraping noise, an excruciating uproar, a gut-wrenching din that left the people scrambling to get away from the awful sound, their hands glued to their ears. The decoy quickly closed his beak and watched as the last of them disappeared from his view.

"They hate me." That was all he could think. "I could never be a sparrow."

He sulked as he roamed to another part of the park, unsure what to do next. He watched a dog play with its owner. The man threw a ball, then the dog caught it and brought it back.

"I wish I could be a pet." the decoy thought gloomily. Then he had a brilliant idea. "I'll be a dog!" He approached the place where the man was playing with his dog and waited for the ball to be thrown again. As soon as it was, he jumped up and smacked it out of the air, sending it rolling back to the man. But the owner of the dog didn't seem to notice, he just picked up the ball again and threw it to his dog. The decoy tried several more times to catch toys being thrown by dog owners, but he was never successful.

"I suppose I don't have what it takes to be a dog." He sighed. He continued ambling along. He soon came upon the town zoo. Entering it, he noticed most of the people inside were crowded around the same attraction.

Upon further inspection, he realized it was the otters. They were swimming, flipping, and doing tricks, and the people loved it.

"I know why I can't be a real duck, or a sparrow, or a dog. I'm supposed to be an otter!" The decoy became very excited at this realization. He climbed up to the top of the fence and jumped into the otter enclosure. He started copying the otters, swimming, flipping, and doing tricks, just like them. But instead of treating him like the otters, the people began to look confused, and the zookeeper came to see what was wrong.

"Now how did that get in there?" the zookeeper exclaimed. "You're not an otter!" He reached down and pulled out the decoy, setting him next to the enclosure.

"I'm not an otter." The decoy repeated in his mind again and again as he wandered away from the zoo. "Why would I ever think I could be an otter?"

It was getting dark now, and he could only think of one place to go. So, quite reluctantly, he began his journey back to the pond. "I'm just a sad, useless lump of plastic. I'll never be more than that." Those were words that went through his mind all the way back. Those were the words that were going through his mind once again when he noticed the park ranger searching the park desperately. The park ranger looked up and noticed the decoy.

"There you are!" He practically shouted. "I've been looking everywhere for you. Not a single duck came to the pond today because you weren't there. I'm so happy to see you. I've been searching for hours. No one came to the pond because there weren't any ducks. But now you're here, and everything's okay. Just don't run away like that ever again!"

The park ranger picked him up and carefully washed away all the dirt and grime that he'd gathered that day. He gently placed the decoy back in the pond and smiled kindly as he said good night.

The decoy spent the night pondering what the park ranger had said. No one had come to the pond that day, because no ducks had come, because he wasn't there. The park ranger had been so happy to see him. He was needed. He couldn't be a real duck, or a sparrow, or a dog, or an otter, because that's not who he was supposed to be. He was supposed to be himself. That was who the people needed, and that was what he would be.

About the Author

Molly Bilbey is fifteen-years-old and homeschooled. She has loved writing since she was eight, and has always dreamed of writing as a career. She enjoys many forms of writing, from poems to stories to persuasive essays! Overall, Molly is extremely thankful for her wonderful family who has supported her every step of the way and is quite excited about what the future may hold.

Teen Published Finalist

"G"

Erin Burchill

To jump seems the only option.

My arms miss the cool metal touch, the fresh blooms of blood, the sharpness that dulls the pain.

My ears miss the sounds of my family, the AC unit, any noise that can silence the voices. My eyes miss the reassuring words of my friends, the pull that keeps me from the edge, the words that have all gone dark. To jump is the only option.

I'm seconds away from letting go. A breath. A breeze. A slip.

Anything to make it stop.

It all happens so fast. The hiding, the talking, the police, the crying. The drive to see my mother. The talk over the phone. The call to the hospital.

I sleep in that creaky bed, in that itchy gown that makes me feel like a test subject, being poked and prodded for vitals and answers that make my head spin and my scars burn.

They tell me I'm sick. They tell me I need to be fixed. They tell me I have to stay longer, in that bed, in that cold, sterile, sad place, and I don't want to. I want home. I want rest. I want to be happy.

I wait for hours. Scrolling through television. Sleeping away the memories. Aching for my life back. But they won't let me have it back.

Who are they to tell me what I need?

The screams come fast. I lash, I hurt, and I rip out my pain and place it on a silver platter for all to view. And they eat it up, savoring every bite, every taste. They don't care. They don't see. They only think they do. But they never will.

Suddenly I forget, a smile on my face as the drugs are pumped into my blood. I laugh at the ceiling; my mother is confused. I feel silly. Giddy. But it all goes away when I wake up to see the gurney, with all its straps and buckles. I'm locked in and taken away from the only thing I have left, stuffed into an ambulance and driven to Hell.

The outside is brick and mortar; the inside is pain and imprisonment. I feel trapped.

Inside, my comfort is taken, as well as my dignity. I'm stripped of my clothes and my possessions, and I'm shoved into an unfamiliar maze full of faces and doctors and imitated joy. I do all I can and bang my head against the cinderblock wall, trying to wake myself up from a dream I know is waking reality. I sleep off the numbness, starve myself, and don't speak for an entire day.

The norm is socks and sweatpants, puzzles and coloring pages, sadness and silence. Anything happy is out of place. Smiles are rare; mine are entirely absent. No touching, no swearing, no hoods or strings. So many rules.

It's lights out, but the lights here never go out. They're always on, streaming in through the door that has to stay open all night. Staff comes to check on us every 15 minutes. I have two roommates; they're nice, but I still won't speak. I try to sleep in that itchy gown, under the itchy sheets, in my itchy, scar-covered skin.

My eyes never close.

My thoughts never slow.

Morning comes after what feels like days, and I'm awoken with the best news I've had all week.

I'm handed a paper bag stuffed with my clothes and my books and my soap, sent by my father who I haven't seen since it all happened.

I miss my mom; there's no visitation, so I have to wait until the phones are turned on to talk to her. I want to hear her voice. For her to tell me everything's okay.

It's bright and early, seven a.m., and I'm finally clean and wearing normal clothes. There's about an hour until breakfast, so I sit alone in a big, boxy, uncomfortable chair with a blank piece of paper and a marker, staring at the lines and the green ink and thinking of nothing.

I'm starving, and my rumbling stomach only distracts me from the words I want to scrawl out onto paper. I have no topic to focus my writing around, so I blank again, waiting for something to find me.

When it's time to go to breakfast, we're lined up outside the dayroom, against the wall like suspects in a police lineup. We silently walk down the winding halls, past the door I came in through the day before, and into a cafeteria that smells like moldy cheese and dirty dishwater.

I don't eat much. I sit by myself again. I think about what I could write.

Then the perfect subject slinks into view.

Her name is "G." She's tall, beautiful; she wears tight leggings and baggy crewnecks and looks like someone who would bully me. But she's exactly the type I'd fall for.

I don't yet see her as a muse for my poetry; how do you write about someone you know nothing about? I fill my time doing puzzles, coloring, reading, and trying to come up with a way to talk to her, read her, figure out who she is.

A few days go by—I stop counting, stop trying to remember what day of the week it is. I open up slowly, I make friends, I learn about why they came to the hospital, and I watch them leave. "S," like her untamed brown curls, is unexpected and natural. "C" appears innocent, but under that indie-aesthetic façade is nothing but pain. "M" is skinny, and seems so quietly perfect, yet her anxieties are dark and carving. "I" is tall, built like they lift weights, and has a ginger-covered head, but I know next to none of what happens inside that head.

I'm put on new medication, I'm taught how to use coping skills and recognize my emotions. I'm taught how to fake my okayness. Nothing is helping; I lie and tell the doctors that all of it is helping, and that I'm getting better.

I'm not.

"G" and I slowly gravitate towards each other, and I learn to use words that put her entire self onto paper. We laugh together, and we share the things that make us tick, the things we've done to ourselves. Why we hurt in the first place, why we hurt in response.

We watch movies together at night with the rest of the group: Pitch Perfect, Mean Girls, What a Girl Wants. It feels like home, all those cheesy 2000s movies. It feels happy.

One night, when we're getting our meds, a tech, Chris, doles them out to us. He's got brown hair like mine, and he's barely taller than me. He tells me he's from my town, and he seems like me, too. We're both wild, rowdy spirits stomped on by the worlds inside and outside our minds. He's not like the other techs; he's more talkative, more funny. When it's my turn, he tells me I look familiar. I tell him I'm new.

"I feel like I've seen you before." He pulls up my information on his computer. "So, what brings you here?"

"I tried to jump off a balcony."

He flinches, his eyebrows raise. "Wow. Well, good thing you didn't. I'm glad you're still here." He smiles, and hands me my meds and a little paper cup full of water.

"Thanks."

It's my last lights out, and for the sixth time, the lights don't go out.

It's early, I'm not tired, so I stay up, and I think. I think of what happened over a week ago, of what I almost did to myself. I think of those two days in that stuffy little room with that little TV and the creaky bed and the itchy gown and my mom sleeping in a chair. I think of the drugs, the ambulance, the door to the hospital. I think of all the hours I've spent in that blue room with the colorful drawings and healing words, and I think of all the hours that I've wasted in that room.

I'm laying on my bed, flat out on my stomach, when I hear socked footsteps coming through the open door.

"G" says something I don't like to repeat.

I laugh, confused. "Thank you?"

"That's a compliment. And it's very true."

She flops down onto her bed, the bit of daylight still coming in through the slim windows and the light from the hall brightening up her face. Her height isn't so obvious when she's slouched like this; she looks so meek and scared, but I know she's not. Her signature Christmas pants drape over her legs, and her torso swims in her black crewneck.

"What's wrong?" she asks me.

"Nothing. Just thinking."

"About?"

"This week. It's been so weird, and I really hate it here, but I also don't wanna leave." She nods. "Why?"

I have to think about my answer. "I dunno, it's...it's fun here, and it's nice to not have to worry about things. I can just worry about me. It's a nice distraction."

She nods again.

"And...I kind of have a crush on someone that I'll never see again."

That lights her up. She's interested now. "Ooooh, who is it? Tell me. Wait no, let me guess. Is it 'I?' No...it's that girl from the other room—'A,' right?

Wait, no!" She just looks at me for a second, smiling and squinting. "Tell me."

"I'll give you a hint...it starts with 'G.'"

Her eyes open up, and her smile goes away a bit. Her hands shoot up to cover her mouth. "I knew it."

"What? You did not."

"Girl, it is so obvious. Even 'I' knows."

"Well, I didn't want to say anything in case it was, like, awkward or anything. And you're way out of my league, so it doesn't even matter." "Are you that oblivious?"

I stare at her, and she stares back, amazed.

"What?"

"I like you too. I have since I got here."

My heart explodes into a million tiny butterflies, flapping around in my cavernous torso.

This girl, this girl that is so beautiful and funny and tormented and perfect in every way, likes me back? It's too much to take, too good to be true.

"I—" I don't know what to say to her, so I let my mouth do the talking instead of my brain. "Can I hug you?"

She laughs. "You just want a hug? Well, I do too, I guess. C'mere."

We both stand and take a breath before wrapping our arms around each other and staying there for a moment, taking in the softness of each other, the comfort of being held. When she pulls away, I miss her pressure around me. But I sit back down on the bed, just as she does.

"That was really nice. It's been a while since I've had a hug."

"Me too." She smiles at me.

We sit there for a bit, just looking into each other's eyes. I don't see her next words coming, but they come just the same.

"Since you're leaving tomorrow, and you've finally spilled your secrets to me...I feel like a goodbye kiss is in order."

My mind immediately goes to the tech checking rooms. "We can't, we'd get in so much trouble if they caught us."

"They won't, it'll be fine. Just come sit on my bed. It'll be super quick, I promise."

I sigh, and think for a moment. Do I really want to risk this?

Yes.

But what if we get caught? I can't deal with the anxiety of that.

It doesn't matter. We'll do it fast and no one will know.

I stand up and slowly take the two steps between my bed and hers, sitting down close. "Are you ready?"

"I dunno. It's been a while since I've done...anything like this."

"We can wait until you're okay to do it. It'll be okay, I promise. Just a quick peck on the lips and we're done. Okay?"

I take a breath. "Okay."

I prepare myself for what feels like the biggest moment of my life, and right as I'm getting ready to say the word, footsteps come down the hall.

My brain processes it too slowly to move.

The tech sees us, walks past, and comes back to start the yelling.

"No, no no no no no. You cannot be that close, get off her bed right now.

Is there something going on here? I have to turn the lights on, I just—you guys know you can't be doing that kind of stuff...."

I zone out and let the words hit me, one by one. The lights black out any feelings of comfort and happiness that were here before, and all that's left is anxiety and what ifs and bright lights and the hospital. Everything good is gone.

It gets worse as the tech leaves and brings another staff with her. She tells me to grab my things and move to the next room over, which is empty.

They don't trust me.

They think I'm a creep.

They're gonna tell everyone that I'm a predatory queer who breaks the rules and chases after all the girls.

I get my paper bags that hold my belongings, and I set them down in the empty room. I go back to the other room to retrieve the sheets from my bed, and I see "G's" shiny eyes, filled with tears. "I'm sorry," she mouths.

"It's okay," I mouth back. "Not your fault."

The other room is cold and empty and quiet, and I hate it. I use a spare pillow to cover the nightlight in the wall, and I try to shut my eyes and forget everything that happened, but I can't. It all sticks in my brain like a sour sap, one that comes from the deadest tree. I'm embarrassed. I'm scared.

I'm anxious.

Worst of all, I'm alone.

It's tomorrow, and everything feels somehow normal, even though it's all quite the opposite. "G" and I don't speak again. The tension from last night is still in the air, following us like storm clouds, unable to be cut from the sky. I'm finally able to put words on the paper, the letters popping in orange marker, my favorite color to fit with my favorite topic.

I stick phrases together, rhymes, similes, observations, use everything I can to fill the page. Morning goes quick as the cogs in my mind turn, and afternoon follows. Soon it's noon, time for lunch, and we line up like school children and make our way to the smelly cafeteria.

It's here and now that "G" and I finally speak, at a table by ourselves.

"So you're just not gonna talk to me at all before you go?"

I shrug. "I dunno. Feels weird to talk about...what happened."

"There's nothing wrong with talking about it, we won't get in trouble.

They don't care.

Just talk to me, that's all I want." I nod. "I'll try."

And I do. We spend the rest of the day together, coloring and writing and doing pointless group work. I write my poem—her poem—and finally, in that orange ink, all those words, my words, her words, our words, are there.

"Can I read it?"

I look up; across the table is "G," her legs pulled up to her chest, her sleeves covering her hands. I pass the paper over to her, and she takes her time reading it. I bite my lip with worry, watching her eyes dart back and forth across the paper. She looks up when she finishes, her eyes filled with wonder and, if I'm honest, love.

"This is beautiful." She smiles.

I smile back.

"I" butts into our little moment. "Can I read it too?"

"Yeah, whatever. It's my poem." "G" smacks them with the paper, and "I" takes it and t5starts reading.

When they're done, they've got the most serious expression I've ever seen on their face.

"This is...damn, I wish someone would write something like this about me."

I take the paper back and look at it again. "Yeah, it's alright."

"Can I keep it?" "G" asks.

"Yes, yeah. Sure." It slips out of my mouth immediately. I can't say no to her. Not after I spilled my heart to her twice over. She smiles again.

I smile back.

I hear my name called from the doorway.

I turn to see Chris, the tech from a few days ago, standing there with a clipboard. "Yeah?"

"Time to go."

The words hit me like a truck. I have to pack my things and say goodbye to all the friends I've made. I want desperately to hug all of them, especially "G," but I know I can't. Part of me is so, so happy to leave, but the rest is malaise, melancholy, mourning. I'll probably never see any of these people after today.

But I get to go home.

For a moment, I can't move. The room is quiet. In my mind, it's just me and "G"—the two of us—just like the night before.

Except this time we have even less privacy.

I say my goodbyes and walk down the winding halls, past the other dayrooms, past the smelly cafeteria, and out into the real world.

"G" i once met a girl in a psych ward her presence like a drug, the only one i'd ever smoke she could drag me by a leash, beat me with a stick yet still, worship would her every breath evoke i'd listen to her voice for years she's put me under her ineffable curse her green eyes pierce me, send me spinning mad hearing a lover's song, i see her in every verse her small frame shakes and shivers with vigorshe always says that she's fine, she can't sit still not loving her is the most heinous crime if only she'd stick around—i'd take her like a pill.

About the Author

Erin Burchill started crafting stories at the age of six and hasn't stopped since. She is a member of her school's student newspaper staff, a lover of meaningful storytelling across genres, and has begun numerous novels without ever finishing one. She hopes to one day become an author or screenwriter and share diverse and underrepresented experiences with the world.

Teen Published Finalist

Theories on Shakespeare
Faith Grimmet

Alison Memphis, sitting from his chair in the box-seat, pleasantly smiled over the audience at the Globe Theatre. The curtain fell for the last time and the crowds were going wild. Another Shakespeare play made a new hit in London. In reality, they were his plays; William Shakespeare being his pseudonym.

He remembered the very day, several years before, when he delivered his first manuscript to Mr. Waliegh, the director of the Globe Theatre. It had been a daring move, but one that proved ever so fruitful.

Alison massaged his fingers. He had just finished a short, little play. He quickly reread it several times, his smile growing with each page turn. He had a hard time believing that this was the work of his hand. He situated the papers in a nice stack then went down the stairs, exiting the loft.

His mother stood in the small meek kitchen, rolling out dough for the evening's meal. Three of his sisters dashed about helping with the preparation. With ten mouths to feed, any meal was made in advanced for the meals to be taken at a proper time. This meant that his mother and sisters spent most of their time in the kitchen or washing pots or clothes.

He was the third oldest boy and number four out of thirteen. Since their father had died recently it was up to the oldest men of the house to bring in some income. His two older brothers were successful ironsmiths. Alison was a writer at heart and found little else that he prospered in or could focus his attention on. So far, he had only managed to receive a few meager coins from printing shops.

"A new manuscript, mother," Alison handed her the stack of papers.

Alberta Memphis wiped her floured hands on her apron, took the pages, and sat in her rocking chair. She always tried to make it a priority to encourage her children in their creative endeavors. She was blessed to be an intelligent woman who could read and write. In fact, she tutored most of her children.

It took several minutes for his mother to read through the whole script, but he enjoyed watching her emotions rise and fall.

"Alison, this is amazing! This is more than just words on paper, you bring the words to life, the paper merely holds them," Alberta exclaimed.

"Do you think...." Alison felt embarrassed. His idea was over the top.

"You should take it the director of the Globe Theatre," his mother finished for him, having complete faith and confidence in him.

"The Globe Theatre, mum, you must be crazy," Beth inserted herself in the conversation.

"Beth, dear, I'm a no-nonsense woman, but that does not mean I do not encourage great talent when I see it."

"Well maybe you should encourage a pursuit that actually makes money,"
Beth spoke with firmness, hacking at potatoes.

"Beth," Alison went up to her with his manuscript in hand, hope and courage setting him ablaze, "I promise you that once this play is produced the first thing, I will buy is the satin gloves you have been admiring for years."

Beth gave him an annoyed look, but he could tell he had pacified his sister for now.

"I promise, soon we'll be facing a very different financial situation," this time he spoke to all his family members who were in the room.

"Well then, you'd better make yourself presentable. Don't want the director mistaking you for the grubby pig you look like," one of his younger brothers teased.

Alison smiled and dashed up the stairs to freshen himself up. "See, what would I do without my charming family?"

Alison took a deep breath as he stood before the office of the infamous director of the Globe Theatre. This was the moment he had been dreaming about since childhood. He knocked on the door and waited for the signal that meant he could enter.

"Come in," a man hollered from inside the room.

"Good day, sir, my name is Alison Memphis, and I believe I have something that would greatly interest you."

"Eh? And what would that be," the man got up to fill his pipe with more tobacco.

"A manuscript for a play," Alison answered.

"I got plenty of those," the director responded. "And I don't need another mangy script from a poor boy like you. Now, leave."

Alison just needed the man to read his play and he knew everything would be fine from there. He had to think fast.

"Sir, I think there has been a misunderstanding," Alison began, not knowing entirely where he was going. "I didn't write this play.... I'm only the messenger of this package here. My employer wishes to be unseen and remain anonymous as much as possible."

The man laughed, "And who would this person be?"

"William....."

"William what?" He prodded.

"Shake...speare!" Alison nervously created. "William Shakespeare."

The man gave him a curious stare but headed back to his desk. "Alright, I'll look at it, but only that."

"Thank you, sir-."

"I prefer Mr. Waleigh, then all your sirs," the director interrupted.

"Wait, as in the Raleigh, Sir Walter Raleigh-." Alison began.

"No, blast, it's Waleigh with a W. Now wait outside, I won't have you looming over me while I read!" Mr. Waleigh shouted.

Willing to do anything Mr. Waleigh told him, Alison left the room and closed the door. He took to pacing the hallway floor, getting many queer looks from theatre staff as he did.

After about a half an hour he was called back into Mr. Waleigh's office.

Alison remained silent, half cringing and half hopeful.

"I want you to listen very clear," Mr. Waleigh leaned back in his chair, smoking his pipe. "I want you to tell your friend, William Shakespeare, that he'd better get me a new manuscript within two weeks or else I'll fire him from his position."

"Position, sir?" Alison could barely whisper.

"He's my new play writer, and I expect new material when I order it," Mr. Waleigh explained. "And maybe next time he would like to come her personally?"

Alison was so ecstatic he could barely process the world around him, but he was able to come up with a quick story for answer to the question.

After all his new job just confirmed his mastery at tale-telling.

"Mr. Waleigh, I think that to be unwise. You see, my friend has been cursed with an awful deformity of the face from a fire accident and rarely, if ever, goes out in public," Alison responded. "He prefers to be alone. He has no relations and is divorced, but is quite rich."

"God bless his soul," Mr. Waleigh remarked, his mind obviously imagining the horrid ugliness of his new playwright. "Yes, I can see how he does not like to show himself. Well, then I guess business will have to proceed, via you, Mr. Memphis."

"Indeed, sir, it is all in duty to my friend," Alison agreed.

"Tell, your friend also, that he will not receive his first paycheck till after the show has been performed. Shakespeare is an excellent writer, but I want to see how the crowds react before I hand out any income," Mr. Waliegh said.

"Of course, I shall tell him."

"Good, you are dismissed," Mr. Waleigh motioned towards the door. "And by the way, I'm keeping the script."

"Mr. Memphis, your carriage awaits you," Charles, his butler, interrupted his reminiscing.

"Thank you," Alison answered, getting up to leave, but something halted him in his steps.

A scream sounded from the back of the stage. It was alone for only a moment when, more shouts and yells of urgency and terror erupted from the back of the stage.

He looked at his butler for an explanation but the servant seemed just as confounded. Then the shouts spread and the words clarified.

"Fire!"

Alison's heart stopped. There had been rumors of arsonist attacks on the outskirts of London, but surely, they had not reached the bustling inner city.

"Fire, fire, everyone evacuate!" yells thundered, this time from the audience.

Ladies shrieked and men tried to hurry their plus-ones along. The smell of smoke quickly became thick.

"Sir, we must leave right away," Charles urged him.

He was not one to argue, especially when his life was the topic. He followed his butler to the main lobby, where hordes of people tried to press themselves out the doors.

All of the sudden more screams sounded, as a wall of the lobby set ablaze. The crackling of the fire drowning out the frightened people. Very few people made it out before a loose beam fell in front of the doors, blocking further exit.

"Sir, you know this theatre better than I do, is there another way out?" the fear in Charles voice was evident despite his calm demeaner.

It took him a few moments to direct his mind away from the burning flames and to the task at hand. Find a new exit. Mustering up his strength, as a seventy-five-year-old, he climbed back up the stairs and took another door that led to the back of the theatre, towards the stage.

To his great sadness the stage was ruined and alight. There would be no preforming his plays on that stage again. There had been many memories on it.

"Why do you have to bring me up here?" Lacey asked.

"Because I have something to tell you," Alison said slyly to his life long friend.

Lacey rolled her eyes. "I believe that any other place would suit than this large wooden monster. Aren't you afraid you might fall down a trap door at any second?"

He took her hands into his. "I'm trying to be serious, my lady."

"What is it my lord?" she awaited.

""Th' exchange of thy love's faithful vow for mine"" he quoted from his most recent play, Romeo and Juliet.

Without missing a beat, she responded, ""I give thee mine before thou didst request it. And yet I would it were to give it again.""

""Wouldst thou withdraw it? For what purpose, love?"

""But to be frank, and give it to thee again. And yet I wish but for the thing I have. My bounty is as boundless as the sea, my love as deep. The more I give to thee, the more I have, for both are infinite.""

"The same I return and even more, if thou will marry me," Alison presented his desire.

"That would have been a beautiful line to put in the play," Lacey commented.

"Well, its sacred to me and only meant for you. I don't want the whole world to condense it down to a mere quote or fancy rhythm."

"You two! Get off the stage," someone shouted at them. "The theatre's closed." Obediently they left and exited to the dark night.

"A thousand times yes, my Romeo," Lacey whispered into his ear.

"Mr. Memphis!" Charles yelled at him.

"What?" he asked, a little disoriented.

"You seemed in a whole another world, sir. I know the smoke is getting thick, but we must press on."

"This way."

They moved right in time as a part of the theatre's roof caved in and crashed to the floor. This back entrance was there only chance of escape, going back was impossible now.

They both took off their stylish coats and beat the flames around them, holding handkerchiefs to their noses to help keep the smoke out of their nasal passages.

Yet despite the blaring heat and sound of cackling wood, his mind was focused on the love of his life. The one he claimed to love so much had left him. Divorced him, because his love for her had spread into other things.

Women, plays, and his ego.

"I'm sorry, Lacey," he mumbled under his breath. It saddened him that it took this fire to make him realize how much he missed her.

"It should just be through this hallway," Alison shouted at Charles.

Rounding the corner, the hallway was like a severe obstacle course. The fire had engulfed it and many of the beams had fallen across their path.

Alison cursed under his breath, hopelessness beginning to choke him more than the smoke.

"We can do this, sir," his butler encouraged.

Charles positioned himself as the lead. He wacked his coat on the beams and the walls that were still intact. Alison had no choice but to follow him.

He tried to smack the flames away with his coat, but he could barely walk; he was so weak. He coughed into his handkerchief, his lungs longing for something that wasn't burning.

His vision began to reel and he felt the ground underneath him shift.

Before he knew it, he was face down on the ground, a burning sensation attacking his face. He wanted to cry in pain, but he had very little oxygen to do so. Instead, his mind took him to a happier place.

Beth was in the kitchen boiling water for the afternoon tea. Alison came up behind her and startled her.

"Alison!" she shouted.

"Here," he presented her with a paper wrapped parcel.

Beth gave him a small smile and tore the wrappings off. Once she got to the gloves she paused and looked like she was about to cry. "Alison....."

She tackled him in a hug.

"I always keep my promises," Alison reminded his sister.

"Thank you so much, but where will I wear them?"

"Sometimes we need frivolous things in our lives to make the everyday seem like a luxury."

Beth responded with another hug, "I'm sorry for doubting you. You're an amazing writer regardless of how much money you make."

"Alison, where's my gloves?" Martha, his little six-year-old sister asked.

He squatted down to her level, "Soon, all my sisters will have pretty satin gloves, but first we have to pay off a few family things, then I'll take you shopping."

"You promise?"

"I promise."

How many promises had he broken to his family? Before the fame set in, he saw himself as the family's financial savior. He would move them all to a lovely house in the country and they would have every need cared for.

He had started out that way, paying off his parents' debt. But as the name William Shakespeare grew, his family became less and less important to him. To the point where he all but forgot about them, between the parties and his writings.

Each promise not kept turned into regret. He was now a lonely old man, with no one to care for him but the ones he paid for their assistance.

Alison woke up. His body hurt, especially his face. He tried to call for help, but his throat was unresponsive. All he could was lay there, a messy past to haunt him, a present pain to keep him company, and a dull future to look forward to.

"Thank goodness," a voice sighed. It sounded like Charles.

It had been hours since Alison had woken, and was overjoyed to hear something besides his own heart beating.

"You're alive," Charles smiled at him.

He opened his mouth, but nothing came out.

"Water, yes," Charles poured him a cup, and helped him drink it.

The water poured down his throat like never before, reviving his vocal cords.

"Thank you," he rasped out.

"Rest your voice, sir," his butler commanded. "I'm sure you are wondering what happened?"

Alison contacted Charles with his eyes, urging him to go on.

"You fainted as we were trying to get through the hallway to the back exit. Thankfully I was keeping an eye on you. I was able to carry you out of the burning building. I will not lie; it was the hardest thing I have done in my life. I was able to get our carriage and we rushed you home fast. Once there, we got your personal doctor to work on you right away. I'm afraid it will take awhile for you to recover from all the smoke and fall."

Charles took a long pause, as if trying to find the right words.

"Mr. Memphis, what I am about to tell you, might be truly upsetting and unbelievable.....But when you fell in the hallway, I'm afraid I could not get to you in time before some of the flames took to your face. Thankfully though, they did not do a lot of damage. But from your side of your chin to a little way past your ear, you have a burn. I'm afraid that it is of the type that will not go away."

Alison swallowed slowly, a tremor in his jaw started. He tried to calm his nerves.

Charles got up to leave. "I'll give you some time to think about this. I'll be right outside of the door if you need anything."

So, this was to be his end? He was to live the rest of his years, however many he had left, as a scarred and deformed old man, who was lonely and prideful? He couldn't show his face out in public. After all people might confuse him for his pseudonym.

He wished he could laugh, both literally and metaphorically, but he couldn't. The shocking truth was just too harsh and real.

The life he had created for William Shakespeare was now his. He was deformed, a playwright, divorced, rich, lonely, and miserable. At least Shakespeare had a job, now he probably did not even have that after the fire.

Maybe the life of Alison Memphis had been a play? When he died, people would know him as William Shakespeare. No one would remember Alison Memphis and all his good qualities. Even those who knew the truth, would see him as Shakespeare. Because in truth, he had chosen that life over the one that would have made him truly happy.

About the Author

Faith Grimmet is a seventeen-year-old girl who has been writing since she was ten. She received her idea for "Theories on Shakespeare" from her odd admiration of historical conspiracy theories. She is the oldest of eleven siblings, who also double as her fan club, is homeschooled, and a part time college student. She loves garlic bread, reading, sarcastic comments, and studying theology.

Youth Judges' Choice Winner

Unending Love
Sevie Roddy

May 2, 2099, 5:37 PM

Sunlight filtered through the leaves of tall oak trees, leaving dappled shadows across the ground. Cardinals twittered in the treetops, and the air smelled of flowers and grass. However, the sunny day contrasted with Rayla Ranchfort's mood. Rayla lay down on the ground, not caring that the dirt might ruin her clothes. Nothing mattered now that Luna was gone.

Rayla could not believe that her puppy was dead. When she had found Luna downstairs, the dog's wavy white fur had been cold and her eyes had been closed. Rayla tried to revive Luna with peanut butter, her favorite food.

It didn't work.

"Rayla? It's time to come in," Mrs. Ranchfort's voice came from a window.

Rayla wiped her eyes with her sleeve, then took out her ponytail so her dark brown hair hid her face.

"Okay, I'll be right there."

Rayla stood up and stumbled back to the door, head down and hands stuffed deep in her pockets.

May 2, 2099, 9:17 PM

"Good night, sleep tight, don't let the bedbugs bite!" Mr. Ranchfort called as he closed the bedroom door.

"Good night," Rayla murmured, tucked deep in her nest of blankets.

Rayla waited till his footsteps faded away before she turned on her flashlight and walked over to her bedroom wall covered with pictures of Luna. There were pictures of Luna sleeping, eating, playing, doing tricks, and being goofy. Tears welled up in Rayla's eyes as she remembered Luna.

She crawled back into bed and turned off her flashlight. Yesterday, she could've pulled Luna into bed beside her. Now, she only had memories.

In her mind's eye, she saw Luna's floppy, velvety ears, her perpetually wet nose, and her big poopy eyes. She heard Luna's loud, high-pitched bark.

She smelled her dog's fur: it smelled of fresh grass, laundry detergent, and woodchips. She felt Luna's soft, silken fur and wet, raspy tongue.

"Luna, where are you?" She whispered. "Luna, come back to me!"

She felt darkness swallowing her up. She was falling into a void of grief. Her feelings felt like waves crashing into her with tremendous force.

Rayla clawed at her sheets. She couldn't breathe; she didn't know which way was up or down. Monsters were coming for her.

Rayla thrashed, trying to get away from the monsters, the waves, and the void of sadness. The suffering was excruciating.

"Luna!"

As swiftly as the waves of emotions had come, they abandoned Rayla.

She felt like the monsters had torn a hole in her heart and left an ocean of suffering to replace it.

May 3, 2099, 12:03 PM

Rayla spent her lunch break in the bathroom stall, crying. Oh, why had her teacher asked her why she was crying? Why had Noelle made her science project about her dog? Why was everything reminding Rayla of Luna? Rayla hunched over, hugging her knees to her chest, and sobbed silently.

"Oh my gosh, did you see Rayla?" It was Katrina, the meanest girl in all of sixth grade. "She was literally crying. Her eyes were all red and puffy; it was gross. What a baby!"

"Yeah," Kathy, one of Katrina's friends, agreed. "I cannot believe she was crying during school."

"It was kind of funny, though," Leonora snorted. "She was trying to do her English assignment while bawling."

Rayla bristled. If only Luna were here! Her dog would teach the mean girls a lesson. "Ha! And do you know what she was even crying about?" Asked Katrina.

"No," the other girls replied.

"It was a puppy!" Katrina guffawed. "I hear her talking to Mr. C in the hall. She said her puppy died!"

Rayla had had enough. She banged open the stall door.

"She was my pup and I loved her!" She shouted. "If you think that's funny then you're just robots without any feelings!"

Rayla clenched her fists, shaking with rage. But before she could do anything, Katrina spun on her heel and walked out the door.

Rayla leaned against the sink. If only Luna were here to comfort her. On a normal day, if Katrina and her gang were being mean, Rayla would come home to Luna, who would snuggle in her lap until she felt better. Now, there was no Luna to come home to.

May 4, 2099, 9:43 AM

"I know how to get Luna back," Rayla told Mrs. Ranchfort. "Oh?" her mother asked.

"The universe is infinite!" Rayla proclaimed.

"I think scientists have let go of that theory," Mr. Ranchfort said.

"I don't care what scientists think!" Rayla snapped. "My point is, they say the universe is expanding, right? Well, what is it expanding into? You could say nothing, but nothing is still something. The scientific term for nothing is antimatter, and antimatter is something. Therefore, the universe is infinite."

"Whoa, you've lost me," said Mrs. Ranchfort.

"I see," Mr. Ranchfort said. "I guess it's plausible. But how does this connect to getting Luna back?"

"You once told me that if the universe is infinite, there is one of everything.

I mean, if the universe is infinite, then there are infinite copies of planet Earth, each with only one tiny thing changed. So there's probably a planet where Luna is still alive, right? Do you see where I'm going?"

"Yes, I do," Mr. Ranchfort replied. "I'm sorry, but it's simply impossible."

"What, my theory, or my plan?"

"Both."

"You're probably right," Rayla sighed, deflated. "Even if my theory was correct, it would be impossible to get to Luna's planet with our current technology. I shouldn't have even thought about it."

"Maybe you should contact Mae," Mrs. Ranchfort suggested.

"Good idea; I'll see if she's home," Rayla agreed. Mae was her best friend, and Mae's dad was a theoretical physicist, so Mae knew a lot about the universe.

Rayla skipped out the door. Mae's house was next door to Rayla's, so they could hang out whenever they wanted to.

May 4, 2099, 10:54 AM

"So all we need to do is build a wormhole," Mae finished, laying a sheet of advanced equations and calculations on the grass.

"A wormhole?!" Rayla gasped.

She and her best friend, Mae, were sitting in the grass by Luna's grave.

"How are we going to do that?" Rayla asked.

"You take two black holes of opposite charges and attach them with cosmic strings," said Mae, as if it was obvious.

"How are we going to get two black holes and cosmic strings?"

"We'll make them."

"How?!"

"My dad's a theoretical physicist; he'll figure it out."

"Um, okay, but we kind of have a deadline."

"What do you mean?"

"Well, none of the dogs will be alive forever, so we have to be quick."

"I see. Well, desperate times call for desperate measures. I'll bring my model stars." "Your model stars?" Rayla asked, her face lighting up. "Those are so cool!" "Remember when they were just protostars?" Mae crooned.

"Now they're all
  supergiants!"

"Whoa," Rayla gasped.

"Oh, yeah, you missed the massive star stage. Oh well. They're due to become supernovas any day now, and we can guide them into black holes from there. I'll just have to ask my dad how to make them oppositely charged. Let's go inside."

Mae led Rayla into the house. At first glance, Mae's house was a mess. At second glance, Mae's house was perfectly normal. At third glance, Mae's house was ingenious. Rayla had been in Mae's house enough times to have taken many more than three glances at its interior.

She followed Mae to her bedroom, where the supergiants lay suspended in their tantalum carbide infused glass jars on Mae's desk. Mae plugged a cord into an outlet, and the glass jars began to quiver softly.

"We can't let them get hotter than 4,000 degrees Celsius," Mae informed Rayla. "Otherwise they'll melt."

"When will they become supernovas?" Asked Rayla.

"Soon, soon," Mae replied.

And then it happened. The tiny model supergiants, each about the size of a tennis ball, exploded in a brilliant but controlled flash of red and blue light.

They were now clouds of vibrant light, red and blue and white and green.

"And now they just need to collapse in on themselves and become blackholes!" Mae exclaimed.

The collapse happened instantaneously. The supernovas radiated with enough energy that the jars began to shake. It was blinding, and the girls grabbed face shields from Mae's shelf. The jars teetered closer to the edge of the table.

"Don't let them break!" Mae screamed. "We still need the cosmic strings!"

"Do you have any?" Rayla asked.

"My dad does!" Mae darted out of the room. "Keep the blackholes safe!"

The blackholes were surprisingly tiny. Their centers were so small that they could not be seen with the naked eye. However, the matter around them was swirling impossibly fast. It was so bright that Rayla could not look at the blackholes. But the jars were substantial, and the blackholes were much too minute to destroy them yet.

Mae burst back into the room, carrying a miniature box. Just then, one of the jars tumbled off the desk with a crash.

"Open the other one!" Mae screamed.

Shielding her eyes from the immense radiation, Rayla unscrewed the cap of the mason jar. The blackholes were sucking in the matter around them swiftly.

"They're oppositely charged, right?" Asked Rayla.

"Yes!" Mae exclaimed. "My dad hooked them up that way!"

Mae laid the box of cosmic strings on a metal contraption that used magnetic levitation to move objects around the room. The cosmic strings were in a titanium carbide-enforced, antimatter-powered tungsten box. The box was transparent, and though the cosmic strings were invisible, they were fear-inspiring. They were as thick as a proton, but they sizzled with radiation and emitted high-energy sparks. Using a tungsten rod, Mae moved the model blackholes closer together. Then she did the same to the cosmic strings.

BANG!

The models exploded. Cosmic strings entwined, and the black holes united. Suddenly, only one of them was visible. It was still infinitely tiny, including the swirling matter around it, but it seemed to be a small tunnel.

"We did it!" Mae exclaimed, her voice euphoric. "We made a wormhole!"

"But how do we get inside?" Rayla asked, not quite as enthusiastic as her friend.

"We need to test its stability first," Mae informed her. "We'll deal with the size later." She picked up a tiny pebble from the ground and analyzed it.

"Tungsten," she revealed. "If anything can survive a wormhole, it's this."

With that, she tossed the pebble into the wormhole. The wormhole did not explode, or tear apart, or destroy itself in any way, shape, or form.

"It's stable!" Mae exclaimed.

"How do I get inside it?" Asked Rayla.

"It needs to grow. We need to feed the wormhole."

"How?"

"The same way you would feed a dog."

Rayla's fists clenched and her jaw tightened.

"Oh," said Mae. "Sorry."

"It's fine."

Rayla watched her friend grab small objects from the ground and throw them into the wormhole. As Mae threw in larger objects, the wormhole grew as well. Finally, Mae dumped a mannequin into the wormhole.

"Is that one of your mom's?" Asked Rayla.

Mae's mother was a seamstress.

Mae shrugged. "She has so many. She won't miss Fred." Mae paused. "I think the wormhole is big enough."

Rayla nodded. "Bye, Mae. If I don't come out, tell my parents I loved them."

"That's so cliché," Mae rolled her eyes. "But yeah, I hope you come back."

Rayla nodded and stepped into the wormhole. The wormhole was so dark it was blinding.

She felt as if she were being torn apart and put back together every millisecond. Nevertheless, she struggled down the dark tunnel.

Rayla realized that she and Mae had actually bent the fabric of the space-time continuum. Yet, in her quest to find Luna, Rayla had not realized the one thing wrong with Mae's plan: The blackholes were only models. For the girls' safety, Mae's father had put a self-destruction encryption on the software that created the blackholes to keep them from causing serious damage. And Rayla was pretty sure that becoming wormholes counted as serious damage.

Rayla broke into a run. She needed to bring Luna back through the wormhole before it collapsed, which would either tear her apart or leave her stranded in some unknown corner of space. Luckily, Rayla could see the end of the tunnel. She sprinted toward it, hoping desperately that Mae's calculations had found the right planet.

As Rayla reached the mouth of the wormhole, she found that Mae's calculations had been more perfect than she could have dreamed. Rayla was not only on the correct planet, but she could see Luna. Yet something in her heart made her stop.

The wormhole ended in a meadow, the exact same meadow that was a few blocks away from Rayla's house. Luna was playing in the meadow. And a perfect copy of Rayla was throwing a stick for her. Rayla winced. It was as if she were reliving a memory.

Rayla sank to the bottom of the wormhole. She tucked her knees against her chest and let tears flow down her cheeks. It would be morally wrong to take Luna from herself. And besides, who knew when this Luna would die?

Was this Luna even the same Luna she had grown up with? What if the other Rayla made her own wormhole and came to Earth to find Luna?

Rayla knew she couldn't let that happen. With her head in her hands, she stumbled back through the wormhole, leaving Luna behind.

She was about halfway through the wormhole when she felt the tremors.

They were minor at first, but they grew quickly. With a sickening feeling in her stomach, Rayla knew what was happening. The self-destruction encryption had been activated.

Rayla raced through the wormhole. She could see the end, she could see Mae's bedroom. But behind her, the wormhole was falling apart, falling into nothingness.

"Mae!" Rayla shouted. Her best friend was her last chance. "Help!"

She saw Mae's hand reaching through the mouth of the wormhole. She saw her friend's earnest face. Just a few more feet. . . she was almost there. . .

The wormhole was crumbling behind her. When she glanced over her shoulder, she saw nothingness. Just the blackness of space behind her. And still she ran. It was getting harder to breathe. . . the oxygen-lacking antimatter was enclosing her. . . She was being torn apart.

And still she ran. Mae's hand was right there. There was only one more foot to travel through the bent, fraying fabric of the spacetime continuum.

Everything was happening in slow motion: the wormhole was nearly gone, Rayla's feet were slipping as she struggled not to fall off the remaining edge of the wormhole, Mae was reaching her hand out as far as she could.

Finding her footing, Rayla leaped into the air, soaring over the last stretch of wormhole between her and Mae. She grasped Mae's hand as hard as she could, willing her best friend not to let go. Mae reached for Rayla's other hand, just as the last of the wormhole disappeared.

Rayla and Mae were millions of miles apart, yet somehow, they were in the same place, at the same time. And then Mae gave a mighty tug, and Rayla gave a mighty push, and Rayla disappeared cleanly from the place she had been. Mae, who had been holding Rayla's hands tightly, could now see her entire best friend.

"Where's Luna?" Mae asked.

"Several billion light-years away."

"You didn't bring her?"

"It wouldn't have been right. It would have been stealing from myself."

Mae let out a coarse laugh. "Sorry about the wormhole falling apart. I forgot about my dad's protective encryptions." "It's okay," Rayla replied.

They spent the rest of the day recovering from the shock, and feeling very glad that they were alive.

May 31, 2099, 1:06 PM

"How's Rufus?" Asked Mae.

"Good," Rayla replied.

Her new puppy, one of Luna's brothers, was sitting idly in her lap. Unlike

Luna, he had brown patches on his back. "Are the carrots ready?"

"Yes, I just pulled a few." Rayla felt warmth spread through her as she remembered Mae's new theory. The carrots would draw up water containing Luna's genes, and Rufus could eat one of the carrots. It would be like having Luna back, even though it was only a small piece of her.

Rayla grabbed one of the bright yellow carrots from the bowl and fed it to Rufus. The little dog munched on it cheerfully, his wavy fur speckled with the remains of previous carrots. As Rayla sat in the grass with Rufus, she felt more peaceful than she had since Luna died. And she realized what piece of herself Luna had left inside of Rufus: it was not her wavy fur, or her dark eyes, or her playful spirit. It was her unending love.

About the Author

Sevie Roddy lives in Ann Arbor, Michigan, with her parents and sister. She enjoys writing and reading, as well as playing soccer and violin in her free time. Her story, *Unending Love,* was inspired by the death of her hamster. She dedicates this story to Persephone.

Youth Judges' Choice Runner-Up

Home
Karis Rietema

Something red and brown darts across the dark, green, damp, woods.

I peer from my binoculars while I am in my hiding spot to try to get a closer look. But just as soon as it came, it went away. I think to myself:

What on earth could that have been?

I slowly descended down the tree. Careful not to slip on the dampness of the trunk. When I reach the ground, tiptoeing over to the place where I saw whatever the thing was, dart across the ground.

I inspect the ground with my magnifying glass. I can't see any footprints because of how dark it is in these woods.

"Let me go get my flashlight," I say to myself.

I walk around the woods trying to find the specific spot my treehouse is located. A big oak tree with the engravings of my initials on the trunk, E.J.M. - Ellery Joy Mallup.

My family lives in a small cabin in the middle of the woods. There are no houses in sight if you look from the living room window, just the creek and some trees. Really any window that you look in there are no houses!

But you can see the trees! Lots and lots of trees! Trees surrounding our house and beyond! It takes an hour to get to the nearest school and grocery store! Because of that I am homeschooled and when we do go to the store, we almost buy out the whole thing! Also we have to take this dirt road to lead us to the main road.

I found the special tree with my engravings on it. I look at the sloppy, stiff, letters engraved when I was 7. I took my dad's pocket knife that was sitting on the kitchen table and engraved my name on the tree. A year later, my dad and I built a treehouse in the tree. He found out that I had engraved the tree, but he wasn't angry. He just hugged me and said,"I love you more than you could ever imagine, Ellery Joy Mallup."

That was 4 years ago. Now, my dad is really busy with finding a job and we don't get to see each other a lot. But when we do, he is always stressed and doesn't feel like himself. Now I spend my days alone in the treehouse. I could always be with my mom, but she is always in the kitchen cooking. I do NOT like to cook. It is boring. I would rather climb trees or look for frogs at the creek.

I climb up the rope ladder as it swings in the air from the weight of me. I quickly get into the doorway and in my treehouse. It is small, with a desk and chair, a lamp, some posters on the wall, and bird feathers dangling from the ceiling by string.

I go over to my desk, set my binoculars down, and pull out my notebook and find the next blank page. I title it: Weird blur in woods.

Trying to remember all that I saw in the woods I recorded in my notebook,

1. Little bit red
2. About the size of a rabbit
3. Fat

I can't remember any more details. I think hard trying to remember.

But I can't. So I grab my flashlight and compass and head down the ladder. Even though it is a sunny day, I can't really tell because of all the trees. I try to turn on my flashlight, but there are no more batteries.

"Seriously?!" I scream into the trees.

I run as fast as I can towards our house with my flashlight in hand to get the batteries before supper. I feel my compass hitting my baggy jeans as I run.

But then, I see the smoke.

I keep going closer to the smoke to see what it is, and I realize that it is our house!

The smoke isn't just coming out of the chimney, it is coming out of all the windows and the house itself is one big smoke pile.

Then I see my mom in the window. She can't get downstairs because of all the fire and smoke. She is yelling for my dad and coughing at the same time. Dad is nowhere in sight.

I know that the firefighters are going to save my mom, but it feels like everything is moving slowly while the fire is rapidly engulfing my house!

The raging fire is spreading to the trees. A forest fire could start. Smoke is hurting my eyes and they are stinging and getting blurry.

"MOM!" I shriek fearing that this might be the last time I see her.

I see my mom climb out the window and walk on the roof like she does it every day. Although she looks skilled at walking on the roof, the wetness of the roof almost makes her fall. She stumbles and I see her legs slide. But she regains her balance and keeps walking. Nothing seems to phase her.

She reaches the nearest branch and swings off of the roof. She lets go and drops to the ground and starts running towards me holding her hand to her mouth.

"Oh Ellery!" She says relieved that I am alive.

I don't know what to say because I am so stunned about what just happened and I haven't had time to think.

"Are you hurt?" she says coughing.

I just nod. I don't know what to say. Our house is burning down and I am just standing there. I feel like a total loser.

"Let's go to your treehouse where it is safe and I will try to call dad." she says as she takes my hand. Her hand is hot and cracked.

"Wait, do you have your phone with you?" I ask as we run away

"Yeah it was in my pocket," She said.

Once we get to my treehouse she dials 911.

I go out of my treehouse because I can't handle what is going on.

Everything just happened so fast that I haven't had time to think it through. Ten minutes goes by.

Then fifteen.

Then twenty.

The smell of smoke is getting bigger and bigger while my hope is getting smaller and smaller.

But when I hear the sirens my spirit is lifted. Maybe they can fix this mess. Maybe everything will go back to normal. Everything will be fine. Everything will be fine.

I am outside pacing around in the grass worrying myself sick. What if it doesn't go back to normal? What if dad is not okay. What if the house burns down? What if...

What if's are swirling around in my head bouncing around each other making me dizzy and sick.

All of a sudden, my mom rushes out of the treehouse and starts running toward the house. "What's wrong mom?" I ask as I try to keep up with her.

"Your dad called back and he is on his way," She said over her shoulder.

We get to the house and the fire is all gone but there is not really anything left. Just some big wood planks, remains of stuff, and a lot of ash.

Then I see my dad's white pickup truck come into view. He parks it away from the house, (or what is left of it at least) and jumps out. He runs to my mom and they both hug each other and look at the destruction.

I see the uncertainty in their eyes and I can't take it. My parents are not the ones that are supposed to be scared. They are supposed to be the brave ones. They are supposed to support me when I am scared, not the other way around.

"What are we going to do now?" I hear them whisper.

I run to my dad's pickup truck and climb in the passenger seat. I lay my head on the seat and let the tears come out. I cry and cry and cry. I cry until I have no more tears left. Then once I sniffle and am about to get out the door, I cry more. I cry myself to sleep sitting in my dad's pickup truck.

I wake up and the firetrucks are not there anymore. There is silence that is deafening. I slowly open the truck door and I hear it creak as I step out.

I slowly walked over to what was our house and looked at the sight. This is what I see: Ashes

Mom rummaging through the remains trying to find something salvageable

Dad on the phone with the bank

Uncertainty

Fear

I go up to my Dad and ask,"Where are we going to go now?"

My dad doesn't answer because he is on the phone. "No, that is not what I said!" He speaks with anger when he talks to the bank.

So I start walking toward my Mom and stepping on a bunch of broken things and pieces of wood.

"Careful honey!" She says her voice is shaky.

"Mom," I say softly,"where are we going to live now?"

She sighs,"I don't know yet. But we will try to find something. Don't worry." But I can't tell if she is trying to convince me or herself.

I run to my treehouse and just when I am about to reach the treehouse, I slip in the mud.

Mud is all over my jeans and shirt.

My bottom lip quivers. Not because there is mud on me, but because we just lost our house. The house that I grew up in. The house that had so many good memories in it. The only house I have ever known.

It is all gone.

I stand up and rub the mud off of my jeans. It is all over my hands now, so I rub them on a nearby tree trunk.

I pull out my duffel bag and start putting my things that are in my tree house in it. My pen, notebook, blanket, sleeping bag, my jacket, magnifying glass and all my little trinkets.

I zip up my bag and look over my shoulder. All that is left is the desk, lamp, and beanbag chair. I don't know where we will go now, but it is better to be prepared.

I go back to where my Mom and Dad are. They have loaded all the stuff that didn't get burnt up into the back of the pickup truck.

"Hey kid," my Dad says. He tries to sound cheerful but he can't fool me,"we got an apartment in the city!"

"What will become of this house?" I ask, glancing at the pile of ash.

"We are going to sell the land. It is much too expensive to rebuild." He explains.

"Oh," I say shocked,"well I have some things in my treehouse that we might want to take with us."

"Let's go have a look." He says. We don't speak when we get there. I am afraid if I start talking I will cry again. I just have to get it together. My dad lifts the desk. We slowly go down the ladder.

I walk and my mom is already in the passenger seat. I put the stuff I was carrying in the bed of the truck and I hopped in there too.

"Oh Ellery, we are going to the city, you have to ride in the backseat." My mom says out of the window.

I groan and jump out. I climb in the backseat and look out of the window. I am not even going to say goodbye to my treehouse because that would make me even more sad. I don't want to go to the city while I am baling.

My mom sees my sadness,"Let's see the good in this. Think of this as just one big family adventure."

"Oh it is an adventure all right." I mumble to myself.

"What was that?" Mom asks.

"Oh nothing," I said angarly I won't talk for the rest of the trip. I just think about the house. Our house. Gone.

I stare out the window as the afternoon passes by. We finally reached the destination after what seemed like hours! The apartment building as a whole is huge! But the apartment that we get is tiny. There is a tiny kitchen, tiny bathroom, and a bed. That is it. It wouldn't even be the size of half of our house!

We load our stuff from the trunk into the room. The desk and the beanbag chair makes it feel more like home, but I know this apartment will never be my home.. My only home was the house that burnt down.

I might live in other houses, but they will never feel the same.

It is night and my parents set up my sleeping bag on the floor. My Dad and Mom get the bed. But I can't fall asleep. I keep thinking that this is just a dream. A bad dream. I just want somebody to wake me up. But I know that is not a dream.

I also can't fall asleep because the sound of honking and cars going past is so loud! At our house the crickets would sing you to sleep. I don't understand how anyone would even be able to sleep 20 minutes let alone the whole night!

I eventually fall asleep because I am too tired to stay awake. I dream about the house. It all happened so suddenly. It almost didn't even feel real!

Light streams through the tiny window and wakes me up. I stretch and my back hurts from sleeping on the ground.

I yawn and sit up. Wait where am I? I wonder. Then I remember. The events of yesterday come right back into my head. They leave a bad taste in my mouth like sour milk.

I don't have a change of clothes so I mosey over to the kitchen where my mom is. She is making oatmeal on the stove.

"Did the food survive?" I ask because I don't like the idea of eating food that has ash in it.

"No. While you were asleep I went to the store. I got some clothes for you too." She motions at the bag by the door.

I look in the bag. There are pink kitty-cat outfits in there. It looks like a six year old would wear that. NOT an eleven year old.

But I do not want to hurt my mom's feelings. Already so much has gone on so she probably doesn't need my whining. So I go into the bathroom and change. I may look silly, but it is what we got.

I sat down at the desk."You look so cute!" My mom says as she puts a bowl of oatmeal in front of me.

"Bye honey," my dad says wearily.

"Bye," my mom says and gives him a kiss.

"Where is dad going?" I ask once he is out the door.

"He is going to the bank to work things out," Mom says.

"Oh," I say.

After I am done, I go sit in the beanbag chair and draw in my notebook. I don't know what else to do.

Later we have a cold meat sandwich for lunch and Dad still has not come back. I have so much energy, but I don't know what to do with it, so I jump on the bed. It is a great way to get my anger out even though in movies kids are always happy when they jump on the bed.

Dad comes home later at night when we are just about to eat dinner. He looks tired. So I go up and hug him.

Then Mom joins the group hug. We stay hugging for a long time in silence until dad breaks the silence by saying,"I love you Ellery Joy Mallup."

I smile as I hug my family tighter and that is when I realized something important that I had not known my whole life.

Home is not where you live or what house you live in. Home is who you spend time with and who you love.

Sure your house might be great and your location could be the best one, but family matters more.

Maybe home is just another word for family. And nothing is greater than that.

About the Author

Karis Rietema is an eleven-year-old student who lives with her parents and three siblings in Hamilton, Michigan. She loves Jesus and is involved in her local church. Karis also enjoys baking, doing gymnastics, reading and spending time with her family. She hopes to one day write a cookbook.

Youth Readers' Choice Winner

Elemental Cats
Riley Carey

Book One

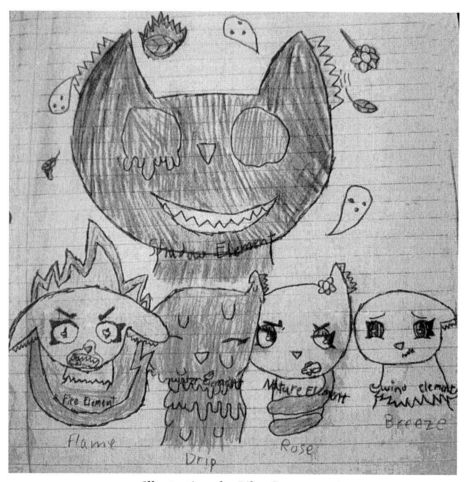

Illustrations by Riley Carey, age 9

Prologue

Four kittens and one cat were peacefully sleeping on the streets near a dumpster. All of asudden, The mother cat felt cold hands lifther into the air. Two men were holdingher. "Why aren't they taking my kids?" She wondered. She started to wiggle. She scrambled enough that the men were only holding her hindlegs. Her fluffy hind paw kicked the shorter man's face,but he still held her. All of a sudden she realized they were walking toward a lab. "I'm doomed."

Chapter One – Fire Element

All of a sudden, they woke up. But the mother cat was gone! The building they slept in front of had the woods behind it. "Should we go in the woods?" asked Flame.

"Ew, no. it's filthy!" scolded Rose. "We have more important stuff, like looking for Mom!"

"Guys, stop being so rude!" Breeze defended Flame. "We can walk in the woods and then tomorrow we can look for mom."

Breeze and Flame walked into the woods. "Com on, what are you waiting for?!" Breeze yelled. "I don't want to get my beautiful paws muddy," Rose whined.

"I like Mud because it has water in it!" Drip exclaimed. "Well then you're disgusting!"

"Hey, be nice!" Breeze scolded. "Lets just go in the woods. Besides, you could use the mud for a mud mask!" Breeze said.

"I mean, you have a good point," Rose mewed. She started scrambling to the woods, instantly pickup up a ton of mud and smearing it on her face.

"Well that really forced her to go in the woods!" Breeze laughed.

Once they were in the woods, Flame was starting to freeze. "Why do I feel anger rising?" Flame was starting to get scared. Then, Flame's paws were starting to get itchy. Her paws were the only thing in her body that was hot.

She felt like burning the forest.

"What´s happening to me?" Flame´s anger grew. She stopped to meditate, but that did nothing.

Did she have fire powers? No way! Power wasn' real! She hummed her favorite song, but no matter what she did, she wouldn't calm herself.

Breeze noticed she was holding back a hiss. "Flame, are you ok?" Breeze was always caring for her sisters, even if Rose was whining about her fashion.

"Yeah, I guess." Flame hissed. She showed all her anger and rage! Her paws burst with Fire! Power was real!

Chapter Two - Water Element

"WOW!" Drip exclaimed. "Incredible!" Breeze exclaimed.

"Show off!" Rose yelled. "You're just trying to show off your beautfy. Everyone knows I'm the prettiest one here," She bragged.

Drip started purring. "Why are you purring?" Breeze asked. "Because we're at the river!" Drip exclaimed. She slowly stepped into the cold water. She swam to the bottom. It was surprisingly very deep! She saw the glories of the water.

But it was getting hard to hold her breath. She wanted to go up to breathe, but she loved it here. Great, now I love the water so much, that I won't go up to breathe! She wanted to breathe so bad, but she loved the water so much!

All of a sudden, she started to breathe! I'm dead, I'm dead, I'm dead! She thought. Turn sout,she wasn't dead a tall! In fact,she was breathing under water!

"Am I breathing underwater?! *GASP* Am I talking underwater?!" Drip was very excited. She swam to the top. "Guys! I can breathe underwa—" Drip was interrupted by Flame. "Woah, Drip! Your fur is made of water!" she exclaimed.

"It is? Wow!" This was a miracle! Drip could breathe underwater and her fur was water!

Chapter Three – Nature Element

"Guys, you didn't let me finish! I was going to tell you that I—" Drip was interrupted by Breeze. "Guys,it's getting late,we should go to sleep."

Breeze said with a yawn. "If you could just- UGH!" Drip groaned. Drip was always being interrupted. She wished Rose would be the one who always got interrupted, considering she was the brat. She swam to the bottom of the river to sleep.

The next morning the sisters got up, Drip not going near Flame or Breeze because they interrupted her last night. They started to ward the city.

Rose saw a boutique. She scrambled toward the boutique. "What a pretty Dress!" Rose exclaimed. She took it to the man at the counter. "May I keep this dress?" She asked. The man looked very confused. He seemed to be deaf.

"Ahem, I want this dress!" Rose said with bold words. The man scratched his head with confusion. "Um, this dress cost nine dollars." He said with confusion.

Nine dollars? What is a nine dollars? Oh well,cats don't understand humans, humans don't understand cats. She decided to run away. "GET BACK HERE, THEIF!" the man screamed. She raced past the hair salon. She noticed the man was very close. Think Fast, she thought. She thought of roses, vines and tulips.

All of a sudden, the man was tangled in a wall of vines! There was the nature element.

Chapter Four   Wind Element

"HELP!" the man screamed. His hair and mustache were tangled in vines.

"Woah, Rose, you have a vine wrapped around you!" Drip exclaimed. "There is? WOW! I'm getting prettier by the second!" Rose bragged.

"Stop bragging about your fashion, and just help us find mom!" Breeze scolded. Even though Breeze didn'thave powers,she wanted to form a hurricane.

It was weird,considering she was always kind and shy. When a gust of wind passed by, her whiskers quivered with excitemen t. Every other cold or warm front that passed by, Breeze always got excited. She normally wasn't all that excited about the wind. Once they got into the woods to go to sleep, they noticed a tornado near a lab! "TORNADO! RUN!" Rose screamed. Flame was so scared she had to huddle close to her sister Rose, their warm pelts touching.

Breeze calmly and slowly walked toward the tornado. "BREEZE, WHAT ARE YOU DOING?!" Flame yelled in a worried voice. "YOU'RE GONNA KILL YOURSELF!!!" Flame ran toward her sister. Breeze gently put her paw in the tornado. She sucked in the air – more like sucked in the whole tornado! Her pelt glowing, she levitated. She slowly came down from the air.

Chapter Five – The Shadow Element

All of a sudden, the tabby busted out! "M-Mom?" Breeze stuttered. The cat didn't seem to hear. The tabby hissed madly. It had three leaves and one flower floating around it. Breeze quickly grabbed all of the leaves and the flower she ran toward the sisters.

"Mommmmmm...." Drip was still yelling.

"Drip, it's no use. We'll never find mom." Flame said sadly. "Or maybe we just DID!" Breeze yelled as she ran.

The tabby paused. She seemed to realize these were her kids. "My....my CHILDREN!" The mother cat's voice sounded evil, even though she wasn't.

"I'm so sorry I chased you like that!" She apologized. A black leaf appeared over the mother cat's head. They all ran off and were a happy family again.

The End.

About the Author

Riley Carey has always loved to read, write and draw. Riley has four pets: two cats, and two dogs. Their names are Koda, Gracie, JJ and Snowflake. Riley loves animals so much that she writes stories about animals. Riley has already begun working on Book Two of Elemental Cats, which introduces some new characters to the story.

Youth Spanish Languge Winner

La búsqueda de Amelia
Aubrey Borr

El viento soplaba contra mi cara y los insectos pasaban volando a mi lado, entrándome en los ojos. Escuché los pájaros en los árboles y el satisfactorio sonido de las ruedas de mi bicicleta rodando por el pavimento.

Estaba en una de mis velocidades más rápidas. Agarré el manillar con fuerza. "¡Cuidado con esa zanja de ahí arriba, amigo!" Mi papá gritó detrás de mí. Pero ya la había visto y la esquivé.

Era un típico paseo en bicicleta al mediodía en un día de verano, atravesando el sendero en el bosque, con mi papá corriendo detrás de mí en caso de accidente. La mayoría de mis amigos asumían que sabia montar bien mi bicicleta ya que ahora tengo 7 años, pero nunca me había interesado aprender.

Hace un mes, me enteré de que habría una gran carrera aquí mismo en mi vecindario, en la península superior de Michigan. No quiero pensar en lo que hubieran hecho mis amigos si yo no participaba.

Pero esa no era la verdadera razón por la que estaba ingresando a la carrera. Como la mayoría de las personas que competían, yo buscaba la victoria, el premio peso en monedas metálicas. Además, como la mayoría de la gente, yo también tenía algo en mente y para lo que quería usar el premio. La mayoría de las personas en la Península Superior tienen árboles cerca de su casa o en su propiedad, y yo tengo un roble de mi patio trasero.

Ha sido mi sueño durante años desde que nos mudamos aquí, el construir una casa en ese árbol, pero nunca habíamos tenido el dinero. Esta era mi oportunidad.

Empecé a acelerar de solo pensar en ello, mis ojos lejanos en una mirada soñadora. Eso era lo único en lo que estaba pensando

"¡Isaías, ten cuidado!"

Desperté de soñar despierto para ver que estaba acelerando fuera del camino.

¡¡¡CRASH!!!

Mi bicicleta chocó con el árbol más cercano y salí volando del manillar, y me golpeé la cabeza contra el suelo del bosque. Mi papá llegó corriendo al bosque, pero yo estaba demasiado mareado para notar que intentaba ayudarme. Me tambaleé sobre mis pies, mareado. Entonces vi mi bicicleta.

La rueda estaba doblada y a punto de caerse, y el manillar estaba torcido.

"Oh, amigo, ¿estás bien?" Preguntó mi papá.

"Creo que sí ..." dije haciendo una mueca. Saboree sangre en mi boca.

"Pero mi bicicleta no está bien."

"Podemos arreglarlo, estoy seguro. No te preocupes por eso."

Todavía no le había dicho a mi papá lo que planeaba hacer con el dinero, no quería preocuparlo con el costo. Además, no estoy seguro lo que el pensaría acerca de mis planes, pero probablemente los suyos no incluían una casa en el árbol. "Digamos que hemos practicado suficiente por hoy."

Dijo mi papá, y trató de levantar mi bicicleta rota y ayudarme a caminar al mismo tiempo. Debido a esto, varias veces dejó caer la bicicleta en la acera y nos sentamos a pensar cómo llevar la bicicleta al auto.

En ese momento, se nos acercó un hombre vestido con ropa vieja y gastada y sin zapatos. Tenía el pelo curtido y el rostro arrugado, y la clase de ojos tristes que se ven en las personas sin hogar.

"Oye", dijo. "¿Necesitan ayuda con esto?"

"Eso sería bueno", dijo mi papá, mientras yo le daba una sonrisa.

"Por lo que vi, tuviste un gran accidente allí". Él dijo. "¿Entrenando para algo?"

"Sí, para la carrera que viene a la ciudad", dije. "Todavía estoy aprendiendo, como puedes ver."

"Seguro. También para mí fue difícil. Sigue practicando. Ya lo aprenderás."

Hablamos el resto del camino de regreso al auto, yo, mi papá y el hombre. Cuando llegamos allí, mi papá me ayudó a sentarme y se subió.

Bajó la ventanilla de su vieja camioneta mientras el hombre cargaba mi bicicleta para ponerla en la parte de atrás.

"Muchas gracias", dijo mi papa.

"Sí, sí, no hay problema. Buena suerte en la carrera, grandullón." Me miró desde el asiento trasero con una sonrisa. "Mejórate"

"Gracias." Dije. Estaba un poco avergonzado.

Mi papá puso en marcha la camioneta y el hombre se alejó hacia quién sabe dónde, pero me di cuenta de que no iba a una casa. El hombre no tenía hogar, estaba seguro. Pero algo en él hizo que yo no quisiera dejarlo ir ...

Lo miré con tristeza hasta que doblamos la esquina y luego, desapareció.

Las siguientes semanas, mientras andaba por el sendero en el bosque, pensaba cada vez menos en la casa del árbol y cada vez más en el hombre sin casa. Todos los días esperaba volver a verlo en el bosque, pero nunca lo vi. Choqué un par de veces, tratando de buscarlo, pero nunca lo encontré.

Empecé a ir allí cada vez más, dos o tres veces al día, dejando de hacer cosas que normalmente hacia como ir a jugar con mis amigos.

No sabía por qué tenía tantas ganas de volver a verlo, pero era como una fuerza invisible que nos conectaba ... o algo cursi como eso ... no lo sé.

La mayoría de los niños estarán contentos de tomar lo que sucedió como un buen recuerdo, pero yo no podía entenderlo.

Probablemente era solo curiosidad; Había leído libros sobre cosas como esta todo el tiempo. Y, además, también me disfrutaba de montar en mi bicicleta.

Pero como el tiempo no se detiene, y solo faltaba una semana para la carrera.

Fue entonces cuando me encontré con mis amigos. "Oye, Isaías."

"Oh hola-

"¡¿Dónde has estado!?"

"Por allí. Andando en mi bicicleta. Por el ...

"El sendero en el bosque, sí, lo sabemos. Vas allí todos los días, como tres veces. SIN PREGUNTARNOS NI NADA. ¡Ni siquiera nos has hablado en.... como una semana! Y la carrera no es sino hasta dos semanas todavía."

"Diez días." Aclaré yo

"No me salgas con tus cosas de nerd, hermano. Solo quiero que vuelvas a ser nuestro amigo." replico uno de mis amigos.

"¡Sí, soy tu amigo!" Reclame.

"Bueno, en realidad no. Los amigos hablan entre sí. Y tú....

"Quiero ganar la carrera, ¿de acuerdo?" - exclamé yo

"¡YO TAMBIÉN! Pero también quiero que todos seamos amigos y pasemos el rato y esas cosas." dijo otro.

"¡Podemos hacer eso luego de que gane la carrera!"

"¿Tu, ganar la carrera? Pregunto alguien-¡Pero si apenas acabas de aprender a montar!"

"Sí, pero como habrás notado, voy al sendero, ¡como 3 veces al día!"

"Eres tan gracioso." Respondió, pero note empezaba a enojarse.

"Lo siento, ¿de acuerdo? Pasaré más tiempo ustedes."

"Está bien, nosotros ... está bien...deberías..." Todavía parecía frustrado.

"Mejor me voy"

Empecé a andar en bicicleta solo una vez al día y luego a tratar de pasar el rato con mis amigos, pero resulta que ellos nunca estaban en casa o no estaban disponibles, lo cual era bastante sospechoso. Me preocupé un poco por eso, pero traté de no pensar demasiado en eso.

Concéntrate en la carrera- me dije- Y eso es lo que traté de hacer, pero, con aquello que habían dicho mis amigos y el pensando en del hombre sin casa, simplemente no podía concentrarme.

Empecé a estrellarme cada vez más y empecé a llorar hasta quedarme dormido cada noche. Realmente me estaba estresando.

Unos días antes de la carrera, mi papá se dio cuenta. Había perdido el equilibrio por la ira y la frustración, y me caí al costado del camino. "Amigo, ¿qué te está pasando?" Preguntó mi papá.

Las lágrimas comenzaron a brotar de mis ojos.

"Yo … no sé …" y ahora sí que caían lagrimas a chorros por mi rostro y me sentí como un bebé sentado allí. Mi papá parado frente a mí me miraba con una expresión preocupada en su rostro, mientras yo pensaba en los amigos que estaban enojados y el hombre que nos ayudó… que no tenía casa…

Mi papá me llevó de regreso al auto, sin mi bicicleta, y me dejó en el auto solo, llorando, mientras él iba a buscar mi bicicleta al camino. Lloré y lloré hasta que olvidé por qué lloraba, y cuando al fin recordé y me di cuenta de que estaba llorando sin razón alguna.

Me calmé una vez que mi papá regresó a la vieja camioneta y cargó mi bicicleta en la parte de atrás. Me quedé dormido una vez que comenzamos a movernos.

Desperté en medio de la noche. Recordé lo que había sucedido y me sentí un poco avergonzado, pero estaba demasiado cansado para preocuparme tanto. Agradecí que mis padres me hubieran acostado y miré el reloj para ver qué hora era. Cinco en punto. Había dormido la mitad del día y toda la noche, y ahora aquí estaba. Pensé en lo que había sucedido el día anterior. Realmente necesitaba aplicar mi cabeza al juego.

Decidí leer para calmar mis pensamientos, pero solo ayudó un poco, porque mi mente quería seguir divagando.

Puaj.

Me levanté, me vestí, fui al baño y bajé las escaleras. Me senté en la cocina y apoyé la cara en la fría encimera, tratando de calmar mi mente acelerada. Eso ayudó un poco. Me quedé allí un rato, escuchando el zumbido del reloj y el frigorífico. El sol comenzó a salir lentamente cuando mi mamá bajó las escaleras.

"Buenos días." dijo, no respondí - "Papá me contó lo que … pasó. ¿Estás bien?

¿Necesitas decirnos algo? " "No sé," murmuré.

"Cariño, no quiero que esto vuelva a suceder. Dime qué te molesta." "Supongo que solo estoy estresado".

"Entiendo," dijo. "¿Hay algo que podamos hacer para ayudar?" "Creo que solo necesito descansar".

"Sí." Respondió ella

Y eso fue lo que hice el resto del día y el día siguiente. Luego comencé a trabajar en mi bicicleta nuevamente y a concentrarme. Empecé a ganar velocidad y a mejorar en la forma de esquivar obstáculos, tanto mejoré que mi papa ya no podía seguirme.

Solo faltaban tres días para la carrera. Empezó a llegar gente de la península inferior, incluso de Detroit, Grand Rapids y Lansing. Incluso algunos niños vinieron del Canadá. El día antes de la carrera, mi papá y yo fuimos a inscribirnos. Vi a muchos niños, de 7 a 9 años, haciendo fila.

Cuando llegamos al mostrador, la señora dijo que nos habíamos apuntado justo a tiempo y que solo quedaban unos pocos espacios. Me sorprendió bastante, ya que se suponía que había alrededor de doscientos cupos.

Apenas pude dormir esa noche. Me quedé dormido pensando en la casa del árbol que iba a construir y soñé con eso toda la noche.

Por fin llegó el día de la carrera. Estaba muy nervioso. Traté de componerme y sentirme feliz, ya que era esto por lo que había pasado semanas preparándome. Pero como ocurre en este tipo de cosas, no importa cuánto trate, continuaba estando nervioso ¿te imaginas? Hoy era el día.

Condujimos hasta el sendero, luchamos por encontrar un lugar para estacionar y nos dirigimos a la línea de salida. Encontramos nuestro lugar en el medio de la zona gruesa donde se aglomeraban participantes alineados y listos para la salida. La multitud era tan larga como una cancha de fútbol, y se extendía hacia atrás desde la línea de salida. Al menos eso era lo que yo sentía.

Bebí un poco de agua para detener la sensación de vértigo que tenía al mirar a los cientos de niños haciendo fila.

"Puedes hacer esto, amiguito. Recuerda concentrarte." me animaba mi papa.

"Sí." Contesté.

"Nos vemos en la meta."

"Nos vemos…"

Lo vi a un lado del camino mientras se unía a los otros padres, abuelos y seres queridos de todos los niños que se habían se alineado para la carrera.

El árbitro o como sea que llamen a la persona que da el inicio a una carrera caminó hacia el costado de la línea de salida. La carrera estaba a punto de comenzar.

Puse mi pie en el pedal y el otro en el suelo para no caerme.

"¡En sus marcas!" preparo la bocina del arranque. "Prepárate …" Vi a todos prepararse para partir, "¡y VAMOS!"

Todos volaron desde sus lugares de partida, algunos con inicios más rápidos que otros. Yo tuve un comienzo lento, y algunas personas me pasaron a toda velocidad, pero poco a poco comencé a ganar camino. Pasé por delante de dos personas y estabilicé mi paso junto a otras cuantas.

Me fascino observar todas las bicicletas. Rojo, verde, rojo y verde, blanco y negro y azul, y casi todas las combinaciones de colores que se te ocurran.

Empecé a tambalearme.

¡Pon atención! - me dije

Me estabilicé. Un par de personas me pasaron de lado y yo pasé a otras cuantas. Tenía que estar todavía en algún lugar entre el cincuenta o el cuarenta, pero todavía tenía tiempo para avanzar. Pedaleé más fuerte, pero iba prácticamente tan rápido como podía, pero solo pasé a un par de niños, y luego reduje la velocidad nuevamente. Traté de mantener el ritmo un poco más rápido y casi choco contra alguien.

"¡Oye, echa un vistazo a tu alrededor, hermano!"

"¡Perdón!" Grité, pero se fue a toda velocidad. Empecé a preocuparme.

¿Cuántas personas podrían alejarse así? ¿Cómo podría pasar a toda la gente que iba delante? ¡Había tantos!

No debo pensar así, me dije a mi mismo, y traté de observar cómo lo hacían los demás.

Entonces observe lo ellos hacían.

Todo lo que hicieron para acelerar fue pararse sobre sus pedales y caminar, como caminar sobre pedales. Lo intenté y casi me estrello contra alguien de nuevo.

"¡Oye, hermano, cuidado!" Puaj.

Lo intenté de nuevo, y esta vez fui capaz de estabilizarse y me dio control y velocidad. Pasé junto a algunos niños más y me volví a sentar. Estaba orgulloso de mi mismo. ¡Había aprendido algo!

¡Podría ganar!

Me había distraído de nuevo y casi chocó con otra persona. "¡Oye, cuidado!" En serio…

Me levanté de nuevo y pasé a otro niño. Necesitaba empezar a ganar más terreno.

Aceleré entre dos personas una al lado de la otra que parecían tener una conversación alegre, y que no parecían realmente estar compitiendo.

¡Alguien se había estrellado! Lo miré, pero no pude ayudar; Era mejor seguir y buscar ayuda cuando llegué a la línea de meta.

Habíamos llegado a la mitad de la carrera y el resto transcurrió sin incidentes. Acelerar, pasar gente, esquivar bicicletas y obstáculos físicos.

Pasé por delante de diez personas, pero todavía tenía de quince a veinte personas por delante. La gente comenzaba a aparecer al margen, gente animando a sus hijos y mirando.

¡UN MOMENTO!

Había alguien parado en medio de la multitud, sosteniendo un cartel de cartón que decía ¡¡PUEDES HACER ESTO!! Con letra desordenada. Lo reconocí de inmediato como el hombre sin casa. Cuando nos vimos, sonrió y él levantó su cartel y vitoreó.

Verlo finalmente después de tantas semanas, y AQUÍ, animándome, me llenó de energía como ninguna otra cosa podría haberlo hecho. Ya no quería ganar la carrera por el dinero, pero quería ganar por él.

Fui tan rápido que casi me caí directamente sobre el manillar. Pasé por lo menos a diez personas hasta que solo quedaron cinco o seis niños, algunos de ellos bastante por delante. No estaba seguro de poder alcanzarlos antes del final de la carrera. Pero tenía que hacerlo.

Me paré en la bicicleta para empujar a una persona más, a otra persona y a una más hasta que estábamos yo y otro niño delante de mí, y algunos que estaban demasiado adelante para ver. Traté de acelerar y esquive a la persona que estaba delante de mí antes, pero el mantuvo su ritmo.

¿Cómo iba a pasarlo? Traté de hacer lo del refuerzo de pie, pero él también lo hizo.

Cada vez más personas comenzaron a aparecer a los lados del camino. ¿Sería capaz de llegar en tercer lugar?

De repente, la persona a mi lado redujo la velocidad casi por completo hasta detenerse.

Miré por encima del hombro para ver qué había sucedido, pero había doblado una esquina y él se había ido.

Espero que este bien- pensé.

Pero ahora no era el momento de preocuparme; Necesitaba ganar esto.

Aceleré un poco, pero los demás estaban fuera de la vista. ¿Estaba seguro de que había gente delante de mí, pero será que sí? La idea de estar en primer lugar me aceleró un poco. Solo pensaba en cosas buenas y motivadoras, con la esperanza de acelerar el ritmo a medida que el sendero se enderezaba en una pendiente larga y cuesta abajo.

Y allí, a cien metros por el sendero, estaba la línea de meta, con una persona cruzando y dos personas a punto de hacerlo.

Oh no.

Me disparé lo más rápido que pude, con la esperanza de alcanzar al menos a una de las personas que iban por adelante. Sin duda aquí fue donde fui más rápido de lo que había ido antes, y estaba ganando terreno rápidamente. ¡Los niños de adelante ni siquiera sabían que venía! ¡Todavía podría conseguir el segundo lugar!

Giré alrededor de una zanja hacia el lado izquierdo del sendero cuando pasé uno, y luego los dos niños de adelante. Deseé poder ver sus rostros atónitos mientras cruzaba la línea de meta.

La multitud aplaudió, algunas personas silbaron y oí sonar un cencerro.

Mi papá y mi mamá corrieron hacia el sendero y me abrazaron y besaron y me levantaron en el aire.

"¡El segundo lugar son setenta y cinco dólares! ¡Estamos muy orgullosos, cariño! " "Has crecido mucho y has llegado tan rápido. ¿Qué diablos vas a hacer con tanto dinero? "

Me reía de emoción y felicidad, aunque no obtuve el primer lugar. El segundo lugar seguía siendo estupendo en contra de doscientos niños.

En cuanto al dinero ... Bueno, sé que tenía planes con él, pero ahora sé que alguien más lo merecía y necesitaba mucho más que yo. Tenía algo, o alguien más en mente.

About the Author

Aubrey Borr is an eight-year-old third grader at Zeeland Christian Elementary School. She enjoys writing about her family's epic adventures. Aubrey loves playing with her friends and competitive swimming.

Youth Published Finalist

The Winter War
Ensley DeYonker

"Chyrul has not been this weak in a long time".

"The kingdom will grow strong again, your majesty"

The queen, sitting atop her throne, sighed. "You cannot promise that."

"We have many citizens training for battle."

"The kingdom of Chyrul is still recovering from the last war, Yons."

"We will still triumph."

"The kingdoms of Brimpite and Fitera are stronger."

Yons removed his cap, revealing a head of messy blonde hair, and bowed.

"Queen Yian, as head of war activities, I assure you that Chyrul will be fine," he told his queen. She sighed again, this time blowing her midnight black bangs out of her emerald green eyes.

"You are dismissed."

Princess Sasha arrived in the kitchens just as the cooks began to prepare dinner.

"Princess!" Exclaimed a chef with short brown hair, upon seeing the graceful Sasha, whose blonde hair, the exact opposite of her mother, cascaded down her plain pink gown. "Nice seeing you in the kitchens again."

"You know I always help when I can, Jemmina," Sasha replied, her green eyes shining happily. "What are you cooking tonight?"

"Spiced chicken, fluffy white bread, mulled wine, fruits, and custard tart. Only the best for our royal family!" Just as Jemmina finished her mouth watering description of the royal dinner, another chef approached her.

"Jemmina, we've just received word that the supply boats were stopped by enemy soldiers before they reached the port. We will have to postpone our more extravagant feasts until more supplies reach us."

Jemmina was silent for a moment before answering, her usually cheery blue eyes looking worried.

"We will have to make do."

The food was meager at dinner that night, but nobody complained.

The morning after, a shrill scream echoed throughout the castle, coming from the bedroom of Princess Sasha. Seconds later, guards, maids, and knights alike were rushing to the bedchamber. When they reached the room, however, it was not Sasha they found but the queen herself. In her quivering hands was a small slip of paper. "It's Sasha," She whispered, "She's gone."

The paper drifted from Queen Yian's hands and onto the bedroom floor, and a guard stooped down to pick it up.

"Do not be alarmed when you find my bedchamber empty," he read aloud. "I have run away to attempt to bring peace to the three kingdoms. I knew you would try to stop me, which is why I left in secret. Do not come after me."

"Princess Sasha will need to be found immediately," demanded the queen, her voice still shaking.

"But your majesty, would it not be best to obey the princesses wishes?" Countered a knight.

"She may have requested to not be followed, but it is too dangerous for her. We can gather a search party to leave first thing tomorrow."

The bitter, freezing air sliced through overcoats and turned breath into small clouds. The howling wind whipped the long black hair of the queen back and forth, and when it trailed behind her it was as if the very shadows of ghosts were following her. The snow had begun to fall shortly after they started off, transforming the once green terrain into a bright, sparkly white.

A heavy fog hung over the snowy landscape, as thick as butter. Yian led her army towards the faint outlines of the mountains, in hope they would find Princess Sasha on the way. Soon, however, even the shape of the mountain range was lost in the fog. Though Yian's royal servants and maids had urged her to wait until the conditions were better for a long journey, she knew in her heart that Sasha would be in deep danger if she was not found soon.

Queen Yian was leading her army through the blizzard, with virtually no idea of their whereabouts, when a few soldiers cried out in surprise. Yian turned her horse around to see what the matter was, and she soon found that one of the horses had collapsed, its rider beside it. The horse was on its knees, its breath coming in short gasps. It had clearly been overworked while trudging through the ankle deep snow. Two soldiers hurried to the majestic black stallion to aid him and his rider.

"Queen Yian," Called Yons, who was atop a mare as white as the landscape around them. "We will have to camp here for the night, and let the horses rest before we lose another one."

"Agreed, Yons. Where will we set up our tents?" Inquired the queen.

"We cannot put up tents in this weather, your majesty. However, we can build shelters out of this snow, and if we begin now they will be ready soon."

"Where shall the horses sleep?"

"We've brought with us the thickest horse blankets we could find, so we will have to hope that it is enough."

By the time the fast falling snow was close to two feet deep, Yons and some of the other men had finished the makeshift shelter. It was a large hole dug out of the snowbank, just wide and deep enough to hold the twenty-five soldiers that accompanied the queen. Though it was not the most comfortable for the travelers to sleep together in such tight quarters, the shelter provided the warmth needed in order to survive the long, frigid night.

As they set up camp after their second day of searching, Yian seemed almost in a trance.

Only the shouts of one of her men, whom she had sent to scout the area, woke her from this state. "They're coming!"

"Who is coming?" Queen Yian questioned the soldier who had delivered the warning. "It's an army! They will attack!"

"From which direction do they come?"

"They come from the northeast, your highness."

"We will have to vacate the camp. Gather your belongings, everyone, quickly now."

They mounted their horses, items safely stored in saddle bags, and Yian led them to where she thought she could just barely make out the shape of the mountains again, away from the advancing army. "If we can make it to the mountains, we can then retrace our steps back to Chyrul."

"But what of Princess Sasha?" Yons called.

"We will have to wait for better conditions, and I will need to gather a larger army. I know that now, though it pains me to think she will be alone much longer."

With that, they started the long journey back to the only landmark visible through the fog.

The snow fell faster and faster, the beauty of each unique snowflake lost in the misery they brought the queen's army. Even the heaviest overcoats could not bring warmth to the desperate troop. Soon, the snowfall became so heavy that the mountains once again were obscured from view.

"Men," Yian addressed her army, "we cannot continue. I have made a dire mistake, and I wish no one shall die because of it. The only way to make it back to the kingdom safely is to send for help."

"Your majesty, if we send out a signal, the enemy troops may see it."

"A risk I'm willing to take. We are far ahead, and can move faster with fewer soldiers. They will not catch us."

"But what if nobody spots it through this fog?" "We will just have to hope."

The soldiers busied themselves with building a bonfire, using the flint and steel they had brought. Soon, crackling flames were licking the sky above, sputtering sparks and smoke to signal for help, fed by whatever flammable thing they could sacrifice. They just hoped that their efforts to be found and rescued were not in vain. Only when night began to fall did they reluctantly release their tight grip on the last few strands of hope left in their hearts, until they were certain they would meet their frozen dooms out in the waist deep snow. Then a voice broke through the painful silence.

"Oi! Need a bit of help?"

He had dark beady eyes, almost like shiny black marbles stuffed into sockets too big for his head. Large, floppy ears framed his pale green face, which was as small and round as a child's toy ball.

He was dressed in overalls, with rubber boots on both of his large feet.

"Lost travelers, ain't you? Don't worry, Just follow me!"

Looks of pure astonishment crept onto the faces of the queen of Chyrul and the twenty-five soldiers who accompanied her. If the little creature who stood cheerfully before them took any notice of this, though, he did not say anything. He turned to walk away, leading them to this secret place of safety. The queen and her troop soon found themselves hurrying to catch up, while also fleeing from the dangers not far behind.

"Excuse me," Yian pulled her horse up so that she and the creature were walking side by side. "What is your name?"

"The name's Gobab, but everybody calls me Gob." "Everybody?"

"All of the elves living in the caves, mate!"

"You live in caves?"

"Years ago, we were employed as soldiers for the kingdom of Fitera to strengthen King Drae's army for battle, but he didn't need us anymore after the war was won. We were only tools for his success. He banished us to the caves, and we've lived there ever since."

"And is that where you're leading us?"

"Course it is, mate! Where else?"

The wind had mostly died down now, and Queen Yian's straight black hair now tumbled down her back, like a waterfall of dark, endless water.

Before long, the travelers reached the mouth of a cave, which had been surprisingly close to their camp. It had been obscured not only by the snow and fog, but also by its mere size. The entrance was only a few feet tall, and the soldiers had to duck down in order to enter. The queen hesitated a bit, but the sound of hundreds of enemy warriors tromping through the deep snow in the distance was enough for her to make her decision. When she was in the cave at last, Yian could not see anything in the pitch black.

Suddenly, she lost her footing on the slippery stone floor and was falling into the bottomless dark.

When Queen Yian woke she found herself lying in a comfortable bed, alone in a small room lit by a fire blazing brightly in a stone hearth. As she sat up, soft, heavy blankets fell from her. The dress she had been wearing before had been removed, and a new one, seeming almost tailored to exactly fit her, was in its place. The new clothing was plain, but strangely elegant, a bright white the same as the snow outside. The queen of Chyrul heard a door creak open, and whipped her head around to see two elves enter; Gob, from before, and a girl.

"Oi, mate! Nice to see you up. That was one big fall, but Pip here got you fixed up right quick." He gestured at the elf beside him. "Now then, if you're up, we can start!"

"Start what?" Queen Yian inquired, confused.

"Why, the tour, of course! Don't want you to get lost!"

With that, Gob spun and walked out the door, his large rubber boots creating much noise as they slapped against the smooth stone floor. Yian jumped up, a bit unsteadily, and followed. "The room you were in is one of our guest rooms, and everybody else in your group has a room as well. This here is the kitchen, and on your right is the storage room, and over there are the stables where we have kept your horses and..."

The entire tour went on like this, for the most part. Gob would stop at times to wave at another elf, and introduce them to Yian. For reasons she did not understand herself, she had kept her identity, and the fact that they were being followed, a secret from the elves, and Gob did not ask her to elaborate why and how they had gotten to where he had found them.

"I think that's everything," Gob concluded, turning back to face Queen Yian.

"But what about that room?" Yian asked, gesturing to a small wooden door that Gob had overlooked.

"Oh, nothing special. just another guest room."

"Who's in there? Another one of the men traveling with me, I assume."

"Actually, that's the room of a young girl who came here just a few days before you." Queen Yian gasped under her breath. "May I go in?"

The door swung open to reveal a young girl, whose blonde hair framed her pale face with bright green eyes. She was dressed in a long, flowing dress, the color of a blue jay. "Sasha!"

"Mother?!"

The princess and queen embraced each other.

"Mother, I told you not to follow me!"

"It was too dangerous! I had to come after you!"

Gob stood in the doorway, astounded.

"This is your daughter?" He exclaimed with wonder.

Just then, The group heard the chilling sound of hundreds of footsteps echoing throughout the dark, damp caves.

"What is that?!" Gob struggled to be heard above the deafening noise.

"We've been followed!" Yian shouted back at him. "We were being tailed by enemy soldiers!"

"Why did you not tell me that before, mate?! Hurry, let's get to the bunker!"

Gob led them to a small trap door, which opened to reveal a ladder.

Climbing down the dark passage, the trio soon found that the majority of the elves had already reached the safety of the small room, as well as the twenty-five soldiers of the queen. Many also held weapons, preparing themselves for the worst. Yian could not help but feel a pang of guilt at the fact that she and her small army were the reason for this attack. When the thundering of footsteps above finally quieted, elves and humans alike let out a collective sigh of relief, assuming that the army had moved on. So, when the trap door swung open, no one in the bunker expected a flood of warriors to flow into the darkness like acid rain.

The battle between the elves and soldiers raged on in the small, dark room. The elves had an advantage because of their small size, but they were greatly outnumbered. When Queen Styo, ruler of Brimpite, and King Drae, ruler of Fitera, entered the fray, Yian knew that they were doomed.

The three rulers locked eyes, and a malicious grin crept across Styo and Drae's faces.

"Ah, Queen Yian!" Queen Styo curtsied mockingly. "I never expected to see you here!" Her skirts were the color of blood, and her midnight hair matched that of the queen of Chyrul. Her gray eyes shone with despicable glee even in the dark room.

"Guess you never expected us to join forces to defeat you, did you Yian?" Drae sneered. His heavily tallowed brown hair, the same color as his eyes, was topped with a navy blue felt hat to match his armored uniform.

"Queen Styo, King Drae," Yian replied with an air of confidence, though her heartbeat quickened. "Call off your armies before anyone gets hurt."

"It's too late," Laughed Styo. "The battle rages."

Nobody but the queen of Chyrul noticed when the walls began to crumble. Slowly at first, but large cracks in the stone soon appeared, spider webbing across every wall. The warriors slammed each other into the rock, weapons smashing against the stone. Yian guessed that the added weight from the snow above also caused strain on the cave.

"Gob!"

"What do you want, mate? We're in the middle of a battlefield, so make it quick," He answered, grappling with a Brimpite soldier.

"I need you to gather the elves and my men. We have to vacate the bunker"

"Where are we elves going to go?" He knocked the weapon out of the man's hands and held him down.

"You can come with us to my kingdom."

"Your kingdom?! What else have you not told me?!"

The elves drove the army back until the battle was mainly located at the far wall of the bunker. The soldiers knew that they had been overpowered, but still they fought. The walls groaned dangerously.

Yian drew her sword and jumped at Styo and Drae. The three locked into battle, swords flying. Though the fight was two against one, Queen Yian fought bravely.

"Go!" Yian called to Gob. "Go now!"

"Let's move! Out, out!" Gob shouted at his fellow elves.

The elves raced up the ladder, leaving the enemy warriors stunned.

Yian dropped her sword and grasped Sasha's hand. Together they flew up the ladder and out of the cave, emerging into the now fogless world of shimmering snow, just as the cave collapsed behind them, crushing everything inside.

Princess Sasha took her seat on the throne beside Queen Yian, on a platform above a chattering crowd.

"My subjects," Yian addressed the throng. "I have some important announcements to make." The townspeople quieted. "After a long journey back to Chyrul," She declared, "The soldiers brought with me to find Princess Sasha and I have returned with our quest completed. Your princess has been found!" Yian paused to let the people cheer. "Additionally, we have invited the elves to stay in our mighty kingdom, and we reward them for their valor in battle against the combined armies of Brimpite and Fitera, as well as rescuing our princess, with medals of honor." More cheers from the people. "And now, perhaps the most exciting news of all." The jovial cheering came to an abrupt stop as the townspeople turned all of their attention to Queen Yian. "The war has ended. Chyrul is safe!" Another cheer erupted from the throng, this one the loudest and most joyful of them all.

Jemmina and the cooks came into the crowd toting platters heaping with food. "Now let us feast!"

About the Author

Ensley is a sixth grader who lives in Lapeer with her parents, two little brothers, a dog and a cat. She likes to read, write, draw, and play online games with her friends. She enjoys soccer, as well as archery, and hopes to pursue a career in animation one day.

Youth Published Finalist

I am Spring
Emma Katke

I am the happy ice cream truck giving yummy ice cream to all the kids.
I am the bright sun helping flowers to bloom.
I am the icy sea ready to melt and be shiny and beautiful.
I am the new ball being thrown from child to child.
I am the excited kids playing outside and saying "nothing can ruin this day".
I am the sweet family having a picnic together.
I am the sad snow being melted by the strong sun until there is nothing left of me. I am spring.

About the Author

Emma Katke is a nine-year-old with a powerful imagination and a love for writing. The way she can translate what she imagines into stories is a beautiful gift that brings joy to her and those around her. Emma lives in Birmingham, Michigan with her mom, dad, and two sisters. She is a middle child who enjoys big adventures and exploring new things. She can always make those around her laugh with her witty sense of humor.

Youth Published Finalist

Found in the Forest
Miriam Wieringa

There have always been four things since as far as I can remember; our kingdom, my father, my brother, and... the dragons. I don't know why the dragons hated us. I don't know why they attacked us mercilessly again and again. Our kingdom is called Luceat, ruled nobly by my father, King Nharus, making me the princess. My name is Opal, and my story doesn't begin in the present, but the past. When I was seven years old and my brother was nine.

Dragons filled the sky. Roaring, giant, majestic beasts that could fly and breathe fire and wanted to destroy us, the humans. There was me, gazing at the deep twilight orange sky, straining myself as far as I could reach on the tall balcony, my peach hands reaching awkwardly up. My light auburn hair waved in the slight breeze, my hazel eyes glinting with hints of different colors- kind of like an actual opal. They reflected the fire that danced in the air, high up above me. My pale seashell pink dress swirled around my legs and my gold sandals scuffed the marble platform.

"Opal!" I heard someone call, and I glanced behind me to see my father, his dark brown hair combed neatly beneath his golden crown. His royal blue and gold robes whirled out behind him as he ran, his oak brown hands grasping mine as he pulled me inside.

"What's wrong? Why are we running?" I cried, struggling to keep up with his steady pace. My silvery floral circlet curved around my forehead, shimmering in the light of the bright yellow lanterns in the stone halls of the castle. Father stopped running, kneeling down in front of me, reaching my height.

"The dragons are attacking. This time the heart of our kingdom, our home. The castle and the castle town. Get your brother and go! Run! To wherever!" He ordered, gently pulling me forward. Tears streamed down my cheeks, and his dark blue eyes glistened.

"But what about you? I don't want to leave you!" I sobbed, burying my face in his chest.

"I'll be fine. Now go find Lullini and go." He echoed. Lullini was my brother, the prince. I raced down the hallway after giving my father a quick parting hug, stopping in front of my brother's pale birch door. I knocked desperately, and the door slid open.

My brother stepped out, with my same peach shaded skin and his dark brown hair wavered as he cocked his head. His dusk blue eyes glittered with curiosity but his face fell seeing my distressed expression. Lullini looked at me, and asked gently, "What's wrong, Opal?" I pointed out the nearest window, my hand shaking as I held it up towards the constellation of fire and dragons in the sky. Lullini looked out and put a hand to his mouth, and whispered, "Dad told you to get me and run, correct?" I shakily nodded and he took my hand.

We stumbled across the scorched ground, Lullini's fawn brown boots digging into the burnt soil. His navy tipped with gold robes swirled regally behind him as we ran, dodging fire. I risked a glance upward and saw catapults pulling dragons down to the ground, and their angry roars echoed in my ears. But Lullini kept pulling me along at a steady pace, his face serious. But that's when the fire came.

Fire swirled in front of me as it collided with the ground, and I couldn't see Lullini. I jumped away from the swirling wall of flames, reaching out my now empty hand. "Lullini?" I whispered. I tried again, louder and more desperate, "Lullini!"

I woke up in a cold sweat, clutching my rose gold blanket as I sat up abruptly. "That same nightmare..." I muttered, flopping back down on my bed, my light auburn hair falling like a feather back onto my pillow. Sunlight filtered through my pale mint curtains, shining on my face and off my hazel brown eyes. I lay there for a moment before getting back up and sliding off my bed, onto my fluffy white carpet as I walked over to my birch dresser and pulled out a fancy purple tunic with gold trim and some black trousers to change into.

I opened my door and strode through the familiar stone hallway, the same lanterns glimmering like fireflies as I slipped on my floral silver circlet over my neatly brushed hair that I had twisted into a braid. Then a birch door showed up at the end of the hallway, and my eyes strayed longingly over to where the entrance stood to my brother's now empty room. I forced my gaze away from it and reminded myself, "It has been seven years since the attack, and we haven't seen Lullini since. He's probably dead. No, not probably, is. I'm not seven years old anymore, I don't have to constantly be reminded of that attack!" With that, I stormed past his door.

I breathed in the dry scent of hay and horses of the stables, walking along the weathered wood tiles on the floor. I whistled, and heard a recognizable whinny in response. A smile crept onto my face, and I ran for the last part of the way past all the other stalls to mine. My buttermilk colored horse held his intelligent face out the window for me to reach up and stroke his nose. His slightly darker peach mane swooped up and down as he dipped his head into my chest, his dark brown eyes filled with a happy glimmer.

"Hello, Candle. Would you like to go for a ride? We can grab Luna and Ember and see if they can come with us too." I cooed, stroking his mane. He gave an excited sounding neigh and I laughed, rubbing his nose. "Alright, alright. I'll go get your tack." I walked to a small room a little ways away and opened one of the spruce cabinets, taking out Candle's heavy but pretty gold and purple adorned saddle. I pulled with my free hand for his similar bridle, carrying it back to his stall.

Candle bounced along the countryside, his hooves digging into the grass with the castle towering above us like a beacon in the sky. He freely strode in bouncy strides across the lawn, galloping to the castle town to where my two best friends lived. I laughed as my braid billowed out behind me, giggling and holding on to the reins. My feet sat snugly in the stirrups, and the clip binding my braid came loose, my hair unfolding from my braid and waving like a flag out behind me with Candle's long strides.

On the outskirts of town, I nudged Candle's sides and gave a little jerk of his reins to signal, "stop." I recognized the familiar stone house with the midnight blue roof and arched windows, and I gently urged Candle into a walk towards a wide open window towards the back of the house. Two white curtains studded with blue roses fluttered in the breeze as I peered over the windowsill to see one of the two people I wanted to see.

A fifteen year old boy stood near the door of the seafoam colored room, his messy black hair waving beside his tan face. His almost orange amber eyes stared off into space until he noticed me, his bangs whirling over his eyes as he turned his head to look at me.

"Princess." He stated, looking a bit startled. He held out his hand and pulled me through the window, his dark orange tunic complementing his black trousers.

"Hi, Ember. And stop with the title! You can just call me Opal." I reminded him, gazing around the room. "Is Luna around too?"

"She's reading downstairs. I can go get her." Ember offered, and I dipped my head in a nod, my long hair bouncing on my shoulders. He turned and opened the door to the hallway. A question popped into my head, and I cocked my head to the side and asked, "What exactly were you doing in Luna's room?" He stopped and turned to answer.

"Well, I figured you'd show up eventually here and probably by Luna's room because she always leaves her window wide open." Ember responded, giving me a smile and shrugging his shoulders. I rolled my eyes despite the smile spreading across my face, and Ember slipped away to get Luna.

Ember and Luna were brother and sister, and my two best friends. I normally sneak off to see them, as being royal... well, it gets really boring. At least... with my brother now gone. I heard someone- two someones- racing up the stairs, and Ember poked his head in first but then moved aside for Luna.

Luna had a shade of deer brown skin and dark brown hair that softly waved over her shoulders, and clear diamond blue eyes that glimmered when her gaze met mine. Her short-sleeved ocean blue shirt fluttered as she raced over to where I was standing and threw her arms around me.

"Opal!" Luna excitedly greeted. She stepped away from me after a couple of seconds.

"Hi, Luna. If you both are wondering why I'm here, I was wondering if you guys wanted to go for a ride with me in Amberglaze Forest?" I asked them, gazing at Luna and then at Ember.

"Hmm... Amberglaze Forest is awfully close to the dragon's border, but I guess dragons haven't been spotted since that attack seven years ago. I guess." Ember decided, Luna nodding along.

So there we were, galloping on our horses in a tall birch forest where all the leaves had turned yellow, red, and orange to declare autumn. Sunlight streamed through the branches, and I laughed as I urged Candle to keep up with Ember and Luna's horses, Flickerwing and Storm. Flickerwing was chestnut in color with a dark brown mane and tail, with a white nose, and Storm was a bay with a cream colored mane and tail and white feathery feet. But suddenly we heard a crash.

Candle was spooked by the noise and threw me off, galloping away with a startled shrieking whinny. Luna and Ember calmed their horses and Luna dismounted, racing over to me. She reached out her hand and hauled me up as I called, "Candle, come back!"

"We'll look for him." Ember declared, tying up his and Luna's horses to a tree. We walked off in opposite directions, calling until we could no more.

After an hour of searching, I finally found Candle in a thicket and took him back to the clearing where I, Luna, and Ember had left Flickerwing and Storm in. I flopped onto the grass after tying up Candle, and Ember and Luna laid down beside me. I sighed, and stared up at the clear blue sky peacefully. But little did we know, there was someone watching us.

"We'd better head back soon..." Luna reluctantly said, breaking the silence. Then I heard a flurry of wings and a scuffle of claws as a dragon- a DRAGON- leaped out of the trees and landed in front of us. I screamed and jumped up, Ember and Luna leaping up after me. Its scales were the color of the sun shining through a dense blizzard with dapples of black around its neck, paws, and wings. Instead of spines running down the dragon's back, it had tufts of frosty blue fur running along its spine to its tail.

It looked somehow... beautiful for such a dangerous creature. The dragon bared its snowy white teeth at us and a menacing growl ran from deep in its throat. I took a step back, my nightmare replaying over and over again. It's a dragon. It's after me, just like they were after Lullini. My heart sped up a million miles faster and I covered my eyes with my hands.

"Aquila!" I heard a shout above me, and I peeked through my fingers to see a figure gracefully jump out from the leafy canopy above and hold one of his hands out in front of the dragon and one towards us. "Aquila." The boy-sounding and appearing about two years older than me- sternly repeated. The dragon gave him a soft roar and nudged his hand with its nose. "Don't harm them, Aquila. They're completely harmless."

"Aquila?" I squeaked, surprised at my own courage. I lowered my hands and gazed at the sixteen year old boy. He had short dark brown hair and peach colored skin with azure eyes that kept staring at the dragon. He had a strange black scarf covered in bright green runes, and my heart skipped a beat as I looked at it. Wait. I knew this scarf. I had given it to my brother as a birthday gift when he turned nine. He had it on during that attack, when I lost him. Speaking of that, he looked... exactly like my brother, Prince Lullini. I ignored the thought, continuing boldly, "Your dragon's name is... Aquila?"

"Yes, isn't she cute?" The boy stated. He stroked the dragon's- Aquila's- head, and she growled something at him. "Okay, okay. Not my dragon, she'd like to note. She is her own dragon." She purred something, and he exclaimed, "No, I'm not your human!"

I stared at him, astonished. He noticed my face and briefly summarized, "I can understand what Aquila says. I've lived with her for seven years. I found her in the forest when she was little and couldn't fend for herself. I take care of her, and she takes care of me." He sighed, and continued, "I suppose I should tell you my name."

"Yeah," Ember noted. "We don't know if we can trust you or not yet. You seem rather sketchy. A human, friends with a dragon? That's unheard of!" Luna's blue eyes looked as wide as moons.

"Well, my name is Lullini. And my dragon's name is Aquila, but you already know that." The boy explained casually. I clapped a hand to my mouth.

"Lullini? As in Prince Lullini? As in the one who disappeared during the attack seven years ago? As in... my... brother?" I blurted. I looked away, unable to meet his surprised gaze. I added softly, "As in the one Father and I thought was dead for seven years?"

His eyes glistened, and he looked away. Aquila nudged his hand and he whispered, "Yes. Yes... Princess Opalescent Selene Lightshadow." A tear slipped down my cheek and my face curved into a smile.

I have learned four things on this simple ride through the forest and I hope I will always remember them. Hope, peace, joy, and light. I don't know if the future will be any different than the past; I don't know if the dragons will attack us again. And I don't have too. Here, under these autumn trees with a cold breeze echoing across my face, I know that maybe things can change. Here, with the boy and his dragon. Here, with my long-lost brother and a new friend. Perhaps someday a new hero will arise to bring peace to both kingdoms of dragons and humans. But for now, I just know that I've found the light in the darkness.

About the Author

Miriam Wieringa is an eleven-year-old author from Kentwood, MI. She is currently in the sixth grade. She enjoys reading fantasy literature and adventuring through many video game fantasy lands.

About Write Michigan

The Write Michigan Short Story Contest began in 2012 as a dream. Kent District Library Director Lance Werner envisioned libraries and publishers working together to highlight the efforts of Michigan writers via an independently published book. What better way to interest readers and writers than a writing contest? Writers could create a short story; readers could read those short stories. Nearly 600 writers from all over the state entered the inaugural contest. Author Wade Rouse contributed the foreword to the first anthology.

For the eleventh annual contest, founding partners KDL and Schuler Books, together with Canton Public Library and Traverse Area District Library received submissions from 347 zip codes across the state of Michigan, including the Upper Peninsula. With 1,250 entries, the contest had 186 reviewers to narrow the field to ten semi-finalists in each category. Nine judges—including published authors, literary agents, journalists and literature professors—determined the Judges' Choice and Runner-Up winners with almost 1,249 public votes cast to determine the Readers' Choice winners in each category. Cash prizes amounting to $4,500 were distributed to the winners.

The Write Michigan Short Story Contest continues to be a premier writing contest in the Mitten State. Libraries and bookstores share the goal of fueling interest in libraries, writing and reading.

2023 Judges

English Language Judges

ALISON HODGSON

Alison is a speaker and humorist, and the author of *The Pug List: A Ridiculous Dog, a Family Who Lost Everything, and How They All Found Their Way Home* (2016, Zondervan). Her writing has been featured in *Woman's Day, Forbes,* Houzz.com, and published in a variety of anthologies. She is currently working on a middle grade novel.

ANDY ROGERS

Andy is the author of five books and has published short fiction in *Splickety Magazine, Catapult Magazine,* on *DailyScienceFiction.com* and elsewhere. His nonfiction can be found in various places on the web. Learn more at www.andyrogersbooks.com.

HANNAH VANVELS AUSBURY

Hannah is a senior literary agent with Belcastro Agency. Hannah has worked various bookish jobs including a stint as a bookseller at Barnes & Noble, a freelance editor for scholarly and academic essays and journals, and as an acquiring editor at a young adult imprint with HarperCollins Publishing. She lives on Lake Michigan with her spouse, two German Shepherds, and two cats. You can find her online at hannahvanvels.com or on Twitter @hannahvanvels.

JOEL ARMSTRONG

Joel Armstrong is a speculative fiction writer whose stories have appeared in *Asimov's Science Fiction, Analog Science Fiction & Fact, Daily Science Fiction,* and NewMyths.com. He has also published poetry and literary criticism in *SUFI, Clues: A Journal of Detection,* and *The Hemingway Review.* By day, he is a content editor and product developer for an indie book publisher based in West Michigan. In his free time he likes to garden vegetables, enjoy Michigan's beaches, and take long walks. He lives in the Boston Square neighborhood of Grand Rapids with his doulatog wife and their two naughty cats.

KENNETH KRAEGEL

Kenneth is a self-taught illustrator and the creator of picture books (from board books to beginning chapter books). His books have won awards from the *New York Times*, the *Wall Street Journal*, *Kirkus Reviews*, The New York Public Library, The Chicago Public Library, the Parent's Choice Foundation, the Bank Street College of Education, the International Literacy Association, Amazon, and the Junior Library Guild. He is also a tutor for people with reading challenges, such as dyslexia. Learn more at kennethkraegel.com

LINDSAY ELLIS

Lindsay studies written argumentation, memoirs of schooling, and classroom practice. She loves not only the logic of arguments but also the use of writing for reflection and the attentiveness of poetry to the natural world. Lindsay has a Ph.D. in English and Education from the University of Michigan and an M.A. in Humanities from the University of Chicago. She is Professor of English at Grand Valley State University where she directs the Lake Michigan Writing Project, which provides summer institutes on the teaching of writing for K-12 teachers. Lindsay is also on the boards of the WILD Foundation and the Ellis Foundation, directing grants toward environmental sustainability and schooling. She is passionate about using writing to help citizens to understand each other, to contextualize their needs within human and non-human ecosystems of competing interests, and to collaboratively design solutions to meet global challenges.

MIKE SALISBURY

Mike's fiction has appeared in *Black Warrior Review, Midwestern Gothic*, and *Crab Orchard Review*, among others. Mike is a graduate of the MFA program at Pacific University. He is the co-creator of the graphic novel *The Quarry*, forthcoming from Scout Comics in fall 2023. As a literary agent at Yates & Yates, he has worked with several *New York Times* bestselling authors, including Jen Hatmaker, Jon Acuff, Latasha Morrison, and John Mark Comer. He lives with his wife and daughters along Michigan's West Coast. You can learn more about publishing, writing, and working with Mike at Authorcoaching.com. Connect with Mike on Instagram and LinkedIn.

TRINITY MCFADDEN

Trinity McFadden has been a literary agent with The Bindery since 2020, where she represents a diverse group of authors writing compelling practical and narrative nonfiction, poetry, fiction, and children's literature. Her focus is especially on seeking to promote under-represented voices with growing platforms. Before The Bindery, she worked in traditional publishing for more than 12 years in editorial and public relations roles at various companies, including HarperCollins Christian and Baker Publishing Group. Trinity earned a bachelor's degree in philosophy and recently finished her master's degree in business administration. She lives in Grand Rapids, Michigan, with her husband and daughter. More information on The Bindery can be found at www.TheBinderyAgency.com.

Spanish Language Judge

MICHELLE JOKISCH POLO

Michelle is a radio journalist reporting in both English and Spanish on stories affecting Michigan's Latinx community. She's an award-winning journalist, reporter and audio producer published at NPR, WKAR and other public media stations across the country with experience in breaking and investigative news.

Michelle began her career as a journalist as the head reporter at *El Vocero Hispano*, the largest Hispanic newspaper in Michigan. Throughout her career she has focused on covering stories of people at the intersections of racial justice, immigration reform, criminal justice system reform, reproductive justice and trans and queer liberation. Michelle has a master's degree from Grand Valley State University and a bachelor's degree from Calvin University.

Acknowledgments

For the past eleven years, the Write Michigan Short Story Competition has helped authors share their stories with the world. This has been made possible first and foremost by authors of all ages who put pen and pixels to paper to tell stories of love, life, adventure, pain, healing and more. This year, over 1,200 entries were received from across Michigan, vying for a chance to be featured in this anthology. We applaud each one for sharing.

More than 130 volunteers reviewed the entries this year, not only scoring the entries but also providing each author with helpful feedback. The review process determined finalists which were advanced to a panel of judges who, like the authors, are deeply passionate about writing. We are profoundly grateful for the judges: Alison Hodgson, Hannah VanVels Ausbury, Joel Armstrong, Kenneth Kraegel, Lindsay Ellis, Mike Salisbury, Trinity McFadden and Michelle Jokisch Polo.

We are also deeply grateful for Caitlin Horrocks, for providing the foreward to this anthology and delivering the keynote address at the Write Michigan Short Story Awards Ceremony.

The generous support and partnership of Schuler Books, Canton Public Library, Kent District Library and Traverse Area District Library has been exceptionally valuable in reaching out and inviting authors from across the state to participate in this year's contest.

Thanks also to the Write Michigan Committee for tirelessly organizing, promoting and bringing fun to the short story contest: Brad Baker, Amber Elder, Randy Goble, Janice Greer, Greg Lewis, Hannah Moulds, Remington Steed, Hennie Vaandrager and Katie Zuidema.

Lance Werner, Executive Director of Kent District Library, and Bill and Cecile Fehsenfeld, owners of Schuler Books, have been steadfast champions of this project since day one.

Ultimately, thanks go to you, our readers, for reading and voting on finalists, telling others about the contest, visiting libraries around the state and encouraging writers to put their words on paper to share the power of expression through short stories.

Josh Mosey, Kent District Library
Pierre Camy, Schuler Books

Sponsors

SCHULER BOOKS

Chapbook Press

Kent District Library

meijer.

TRAVERSE AREA DISTRICT LIBRARY

Canton Public Library

Schuler Books
Self-Publishing Services

Thanks to Schuler Books' Espresso Book Machine, we can help you print your book. You provide us with two PDF files (one for the cover and one for the text or bookblock) and we will print a high-quality paperback book for you, in color or black and white. The Espresso Book Machine can print books from 40 pages to 650 pages long.

What are the benefits of printing your work with Schuler Books?

* This is your book.
* You'll receive one-on-one support
* Since you sign a non-exclusive contract with us, you may pursue any other publishing venture that you choose.
* You retain all rights to the printed work, and you have complete control over layout, content and design.
* No minimums. You may print one copy or as many as you want.
* You retain rights for non-exclusive distribution and may sell books printed at Schuler Books or with the Chapbook Press through any avenue.
* Modifications are allowed at any time, for an additional fee.
* You set the book price and determine the royalty per book.

What we need to print your book

2 print-ready PDF files: one for the book and one for the cover, formatted the way you want them to look. We will upload your files and print a paperback edition of your book on high quality (archival) paper and a full-color glossy cover, in any size you want from 5"x 5" to around 8" x 10.5"

We can help you get there

We can help as much or as little as needed in each area of making your book a reality.

New Services:

* e-Book /Global distribution print and digital package: Your title (in print or as an eBook) will be available for purchase to over 39,000 global retailers, and their customers. The eBook will be available for more than 70 different
Ereaders including Amazon Kindle, Apple iBookstore, Barnes&Noble NOOK, Kobo, Sony, etc.) Bookstores and retailers around the world will be able
to order your book for their customers.
* Title set-up:
  * Book and e-book: $520 (includes 2 ISBNs)
  * Book only: $420 (include 1 ISBN)
You need to order a minimum of 50 copies within 60 days of title set-up.
Additional orders (minimum quantity of 10), require a three week notice.
* Epub Conversion: $0.80 per page (page
count is based on the total number of pages
in your bookblock)
  * Conversion will take three weeks.
  * For Printing costs and author
compensation please ask for a quote.

Chapbook Press

Chapbook Press	Short Run	Standard Package	Chapbook Press Publishing
	$50 Plus Production Costs	$150 Plus Production Costs	$300 Plus Production Costs
Maximum Print Run	20 Copies	Unlimited	Unlimited
Page Maximum	100 Pages	650 Pages	650 Pages
Personal Consultation	30 Minutes	30 Minutes	60 Minutes
Email Support	Limited Support	Included	Included
PDF Review	No	No	Yes
Proof Copy	1 Proof Copy	1 Proof Copy	1 Proof Copy
PDF Upload	Includes initial upload No Re-uploads	Includes initial upload +1 Re-upload	Includes initial upload +1 Re-upload
Cover	Basic Text Cover	Basic Template Cover	Basic Template Cover
Saved for Re-prints	No	Yes	Yes
ISBN/Barcode	No	No	Yes
Library of Congress Reg.	No	No	Yes
Books in Print Reg.	No	No	Yes
Sale: Schuler Books	No	No	Yes
Sale: SchulerBooks.com	No	No	Yes
Production Costs	$7.00 per copy flat rate	$6.00 per copy +$0.03 per page	$6.00 per copy +$0.03 per page
Color Interior	No	+$0.15 per page	+$0.15 per page

A la Carte Sevices
PDF alterations (re-uploads): $25 (+ price of proof copy)
Scanning: $50 deposit / $50 per hour
File conversion to PDF: $5
Cover from template: $50 (prepay)
ISBN & barcode acquisition: $100
Amazon listing: $50
Library of Congress Registration: $50
Additional consultation time: $40 per hour
Additional PDF adjustments: $60 per hour

Freelance Fees
Pre-press file consulting: $15 per 1/4 hour
Manuscript evaluation: $250
Manuscript editing: $135 deposit, $45 per hour
Proofreading: $105 deposit, $35 per hour
Transcribing: $105 deposit, $35 per hour
Coaching: $50 deposit, $50 per hour
Custom cover design: $100 deposit, $50 per hour
Page layout: $100 deposit, $50 per hour
Hardcover Binding: Ask for a quote.

For more information visit SchulerBooks.com
Want to talk to someone? Call us today at 616-942-7330 x558,
or email us at: printondemand@schulerbooks.com